Married to a Cheater –

In Love with a Husband

By Bianca Richmond

BRich Publishing
Memphis, TN

Married to a Cheater –
In Love with a Husband

© 2020 by Bianca Richmond

For more information, contact Bianca Richmond
Email: brichpublishing@outlook.com

Executive Editor | Formatting
Nina Allen-Johnson
Creative Solutions Unlimited
Memphis, Tennessee

Cover Design
Travis A. Malone
Prestigious Photography

ISBN: 978-0-578-77621-7
Printed in the United States of America

Married To A Cheater--
In Love with A Husband

Introduction

I'm Maya, the one who knows *all* the tea and tells it
like it is. You are about to be entertained with the lives
of me and my girls and their fucked-up fantasy lives.
These are my girls, and I got their backs -- no matter
how they try to portray their men or their relationships.
Just like any other squad, we go through shit, we talk
shit, we may fuck shit up, but most of all we **ARE** the
shit! My life is probably the best of them all. I am
SINGLE as hell. I go to bed every night with no worries
about my man cheating on me and me possibly catching
a charge because I got into his shit. I link up with my
girls, hear their drama and deal with everyday tea --
one day at a time. I swear we could get rich with our
own TV show with the drama we encounter daily. So,
come on over here and capture all this tea for your
reading enjoyment.

****

British opened her eyes to the bright sunlight from her window and the sound of her alarm clock going off after hitting SNOOZE for the fourth time. "Rise and grind, Bishes," she always sits up and says. As she moved her blush duvet to the side, she realized that she had not heard from Jordan all night. Looking around searching for her phone, she says with an attitude, "That MF better be in the hospital laid in a coma, or in jail and done missed his one phone call." She finds her phone only to see that she has no missed calls, 3 text messages from me, Facebook and Instagram notifications, but NOTHING FROM JORDAN. She throws her phone to the side and goes to get ready for the day.

"Alexa, what's on my calendar for today?" British asks her home device. "Three home showings beginning at 11am," Alexa replies. "FUCK!" British blows and says. As her silk robe slides down her body to the floor and she prepares to enter the shower, her phone rings. She rushes to the bedroom to her phone hoping it was a call from Jordan. ATT-SPAM ALERT her phone reads. "This bastard is really bold enough to be in another city and don't call," she thinks to herself.

Jordan is a broke Personal Fitness Trainer by day and a dumb cheater by night, who went on a trip with some of his homeboys to Miami for the weekend. British unlocked her phone and dialed Jordan's number only for it to go straight to voicemail twice. "Oh, I'm hot," she angrily mumbled. She then opened her text message app and typed, "Hey Baby, are you ok?" That's when she noticed that the message was sent in green and not the blue IMessage. She rolled her eyes and went to continue to her shower. As she showered, all she could do was rehearse her lines of cussing his ass out and practiced getting her mindset ready to put his ass out if she found out he was on some fuck shit.

She finished her shower, got dressed and left to start her day as a real estate agent. As she was pulling out of the garage, she received a text from Jordan. "Yo, my phone died but we are on our way to the airport. Hit you up later." "Damn, I can't even get a hey baby or I love you," she thought out loud. "Fuck him," she said as she picked up her phone to call me. "Girl, I need you to reach out to some of your blogging buddies in Miami to see what last night's gossip was," British said to me before I could even say hello. I laughed and said, "Jordan must be with the shit again?"

British responded by saying that he went an entire night without calling her and read the message that he sent her.

"Oh girl, he probably was buying ass at the strip club last night. Nothing new and nothing to be alarmed about," I said sarcastically.

British rolled her eyes as she told me that she was pulling up to her first home showing and that she would call me back.

"Okay girl. Maybe your first client will be a sexy chocolate man," I said all dramatic. We both laughed. I ended the conversation by saying that it was nothing like having sex in a house for sale.

On the other side of town, I am in my Ikea bedroom set with my laptop and teacup waiting to catch the latest tea. I received a call from Sade as she was heading in to work. Sade was the youngest of us girls and is engaged to be married to her high school sweetheart. I answered and asked sarcastically what the morning gossip was. Sade whispered and asked me if I was alone. I whispered back and said, "No Bitch, I'm getting tossed." Sade laughed and said I play entirely too much. She asked me if I had heard anything from British.

I told her that British called me earlier going off about Jordan's hoe ass.

"Girl, Jordan called Chad last night and told him that he had screwed up," Sade said. She said that Chad got out of the bed to go into another room to finish the conversation with Jordan and asked him what did he do.

I humorously replied, "Hunny, we all know that Jordan is a cheater with his broke ass. British knows it, and all she does is give him the benefit of the doubt like he just made a few mistakes and is learning from them. Anyway, let's just plan to meet at our spot later so we all can catch up on the tea."

At 6:00 pm, we arrive at Happy Hour. As always, Nikki and Toya are the ones to slide away and go to the bathroom. As soon as we are seated, British starts to go in.

"I'm so tired of Jordan."

"Girl please," I said laughing.

"Girl, I am. I mean, I am so damn tired of going through the same mess."

"Heffa, people that is tired don't rest up as quick as you do and go back to the same man that they continuously say they are tired of, not to mention marry they ass," I said.

"Oh, he really trying it this time."

"What? It's not like he done something he ain't never done before." I laughed and asked the waitress if she could bring me something strong to be able to go through this BS I was about to hear from my girls tonight.

"What are y'all yapping about already?" Toya asked as she was sitting down.

"Jordan cheating ass," I replied laughing.

"Oh girl," Toya laughed as she reached for the drink menu.

"I mean, he goes on this Miami trip and act like he doesn't have a wife at home and don't even bother to call," British frustratedly says as she ordered her a drink.

"He said his phone died," she mumbled.

"Yep, and he also said he was heading to the airport and he would call you once he got to the airport, but I guess his method of travel is Carnival Cruise Line and he lost service at sea," I sarcastically say.

"Maya, I hate you," British said as she strongly tries to hold back the tears.

"Girl, just be like Nikki and be with somebody else's man," I said laughing.

"Cheers to happy!" Nikki holds up her drink to toast.

Nikki is the one out of the group who doesn't have her own man. It is always kind of fucked up that she would rather deal with men who are already in a relationship thinking that it is the best because she never wants to be fully committed to anyone. She figures that if she is involved with a man who has another woman to satisfy, it will leave room for her to play tic-tac-toe.

"Well I hate you have to constantly go through this," Toya replies. Toya has always been the one to think she has the perfect life, the perfect marriage, the perfect family. She always seems to belittle everyone's else relationship since she has been married for 15 years. Little does she know, we all know her marriage is fucked up too, and her man ain't shit either.

We were finishing up our girl talk and sipping on multiple drinks, and as usual, Nikki's attention span was totally somewhere else. Over to our left at the bar sat this dark-skinned, bald headed, sexy and handsome guy. He most definitely caught the attention from Nikki. "Well I be damned," Nikki said as she struggled to regain from almost choking. British looks up to see why Nikki was being so dramatic. Nikki sips on her drink and says, "That's one sexy ass man right there." As we were all staring, two other guys walked in and sat at the bar.

"Ok Chicas, it's about time we get up out of here," Toya says as she gets up out of her chair and gathers her things.

"Yes, because I am horny and hot," Sade replies.

As we all got up and prepared to leave, Nikki flirtatiously says that she was going to stay awhile and chill at the bar. British raises her hand to signal that she was in agreeance with that plan and was going to stay behind as well.

"Yea, I think I am going to stay too," British said.

"Come on girl, your man probably on some bullshit anyway."

"Right, so tonight I am about to be on some even better bullshit."

As British and Nikki walked towards the bar, I yelled "Aye, don't y'all forget, we leave for Hawaii tomorrow while y'all trying to be hoes tonight."

British

"Rise and Grind, Bishes! Top of the morning, and we are Hawaii ready," British thinks to herself as she rolls over to turn off the snoozing alarm. She rolls back over and looks at Jordan in pure disgust. *"Ever wish you could just unmeet a motherfucker?"* She thinks to herself. Apparently, British's thoughts are felt by Jordan. He awakes from the sound of his text message tone. "Good Morning my beautiful wife." He rolls over and say as he slides his way down British silk, caramel body. As he rubs his hands slowly down British's body, he looks up to her and say, "Are you gon' feed me, baby?" All British can really do at this point is close her eyes and vision this sexy bald guy she met at the bar last night. She is instantly brought out of her vision when she feels a hard pressure inside of her. Although she is furious at Jordan, her horniness is not allowing her to pass up the sex she and Jordan usually have each morning before they start their day, especially since she is about to be on vacation for 7 days, which means no sex action at all.

After a few good strokes, British is back in her zone. She rolls on top of Jordan and began fucking him as if it is the last time. "Damn, Baby!" Jordan says as British rides the wave. British don't hear a damn thing Jordan is mumbling. As they finish, they both lay on their backs to catch their breath, Jordan wraps his arms around British and ask if she missed him. "What makes you think that?" British asks. "The way you just fucked me," Jordan says as he gets up to put on his Nike basketball shorts.

"Truth moment time!" British say to Jordan as she gets out of the bed to slip her panties back on. "What the hell were you doing Saturday night the reason I didn't hear from you?" British angrily ask Jordan.

"What you mean?"

"Nigga don't play with me!"

"Baby, I told you my phone died, and I didn't have a charger."

"So, you mean to tell me that not one time did it ever cross your mind that you needed to call and check in with your wife?"

"My bad, I didn't think it was a big deal. You knew I was out of town."

"FUCK YOU, Jordan!" British yells as she throws one of the plush pillows from their bed at him.

British goes into their master bathroom to take her shower. As she turns on the shower water, she can hear Jordan's phone constantly going off as if someone is trying to get in contact with him badly. "Aite mane, I'm gon' meet you at the gym," Jordan said to the person on the other end of the phone. British can feel something is fishy about that call, but she continues with her shower so she can hurry and head to the airport. *"I'm just ready to get to Hawaii,"* British thinks to herself as she finishes her shower and dries her body. British gathers her things to head out the door, and she realize that Jordan has left and didn't even bother to give her "goodbyes and safe travels," given the fact that they will be a part for a week.

The plans were for us to all meet at the airport and fly to Hawaii together but because of the real estate life, the girls had to go ahead leaving British to catch up with them later. *"Funds over Fun,"* British thinks aloud.

As she finishes showing her scheduled homes, she finally heads to the airport. She checks her bags and completes the airport security check. While she is heading to her gate with her air buds in her ears and purple jogging suit that is fitting her just right, she doesn't even notice the guy who is walking just a short distance behind checking her out. Turns out, he is heading to Hawaii too.

British finds her a seat next to a charging port and patiently waits to board her plane. As she is watching Facebook Live videos of her friends, she notices this handsome, tall, high yellow guy sit down across from her. She barely looks up and give him a smile as she continues back to her Facebook page. *"Damn, he sexy as hell with them pink ass lips,"* she thinks to herself. British must pretend she is looking out the window just so she can get another look. *"Mane, I'm tripping. Let me not entertain Maya's BS because my husband is fucking up. Fuck that! This boy is fine as hell,"* she says to herself.

As British is trying to control her eyes, she realizes that the guy is checking her out as well. Wondering if she should say something or not, the guy gets up and starts walking to the empty seat next to British. "What's up, Ma?" the guy says as he sits down.

"You headed to Hawaii alone?"

"No, I had to stay back to handle some last-minute business while my friends went ahead."

"That's what's up, I'm meeting some of my frat brothers there for a bachelor party."

"Oh, and Hawaii is the destination of choice," British laugh saying.

"What's wrong with going to Hawaii for a guys' trip?" he asks British while leaning towards her.

At this point all British can feel is her body changing as she sniffs the cologne he has on. She can't remember the last time she smelled some good cologne on Jordan that made her want to just jump on him and start sexual acts.

"Now boarding flight 2522 to Hawaii," the Delta attendant says over the intercom. Both British and the guy gather their things and head to get in line to board their flight.

"So, what's your name?" the guy asks British while helping her get her bag off the floor.

"British!" she says, trying not to stare into his eyes.

"British? That name fits you very well. I like it a lot. Maybe we can get to know one another since we are both alone and have this long flight ahead." He says as they both stand beside each other waiting until it is their turn to board the plane.

"Sounds good to me," British says with a little excitement in her voice. She takes her seat as the guy keeps going ahead.

British places her carry-on bag in the overhead bin and sits in her assign seat. She places her neck pillow around her neck and her earbuds back in her ears and begin listening to her Spotify.

"Ooohhh baby, I'ma put it down on you baby, wanna give it all to you baby. Can you find my G-Spot, call me Mrs. Flintstone I can make your bedrock," British sings in her head while she closes her eyes and listens to the song choice that is auto playing on her Spotify.

"Preparing for takeoff," the flight attendant says as she does the routine flight attendant demonstration. As time went by, British dazed into the view of the clouds.

"This seat is left just for me?" The handsome stranger asks.

"Of course, it is." British smiles and says.

"Have you ever had sex on a plane?" He whispers in her ear as he rubs his hands across her legs.

British give her sexy look as they both lean into one another and kiss. The intimate kiss leads him to pulling up her shirt and caressing and sucking on her titties to licking her neck and behind her earlobes. British tries to control her noise making, but it becomes uncontrollable as his hands enters the inside of her pants and between her silk panties. These are the exciting things British was looking for in her marriage that Jordan lacks to give her. As she is enjoying every feeling she is receiving, she is instantly brought out of her daze as she feels a tap on her arm, "Ma'am? We are preparing for landing, please place your tray table back in place." British looks around and blinks her eyes several times. *"Damn, it was just a dream,"* she says to herself as she packs up her things to place back in her fanny pack.

British is kind of glad she ended up being on a row by herself hoping the guy she had met would notice and come to keep her company. Wishful thinking!

****

"Aloha, Bishes!" British greets us girls relaxing on the patio of our rental resort. She put her bags down as she joins us and pours up a drink.

"How was your flight?" I ask.

"It was interesting," British says with a smirk on her face.

"You found a Cuddy Buddy on the plane, didn't you?" Nikki say as she raises her hand for a high five.

"Uummmm, I wouldn't call it that, but I did meet a light bright who just so happened to brighten all my dim lights," British say as she took a shot. We all laughed and took a shot.

It is always a great time when all the girls can link up and just sit around and enjoy drinks, laugh, and gossip. I am the one to always laugh at everyone when they are having relationship problems, so that's why I remain single. British is always the one who doesn't tolerate any man who tries to play her. She literally has zero tolerance. I am not sure why Jordan has lasted so long and is still in the picture. Sade is the one who has been in the same relationship since high school. So, their little cute asses never have no interesting tea. My girl Nikki, oh my girl Nikki. Being committed to one man doesn't even exist in Nikki's world. She'd rather leave her options open, so she doesn't have to deal with headaches and heartbreaks. Toya is the oldest of us all and the one who has been married since Lassie was a puppy. She has always thought of her marriage as perfect, so the only gossip she ever brings is when it's the gossip of someone's else relationship or marriage.

Dani is my sister. Unfortunately, she is the quiet one. She sometimes is distant from us. She just recently got out of a relationship that left her bitter and heartbroken. Although we have never even met this dude, she claims to have been in love with for three years.

British awakes to the sound of her phone going off. She picks it up and notice it is a text message from Jordan. "I guess you trying to do a payback and not reach out to me all night. Not cool, B." For the first time, British don't even bother to reply to his message. "I don't have time for his shit today!" She says as she gets up and walks to the bedroom window to look at the breathtaking morning view of Hawaii.

"I can wake up to this view every day," she thinks to herself.

British walks to the downstairs level of our rental home to join the rest of us in the kitchen preparing breakfast and mimosas. We finished and prepared ourselves to get out for some enjoyment. We did some sightseeing, a little shopping, ate and then passed by a few people heading to the beach.

Nikki, British, and Dani wanted to go to the beach while the rest of us continued to shop.

"Ok, those are some sexy men going in that direction. I've seen enough of this. I'm trying to see if I can get some sex on the beach."

"Girl yes! And I ain't talking about the drink either."

Both Nikki and British keeps going back and forth with each other while Dani is quiet and just follows them.

"Dani, you have been quiet this trip so far. Come on baby girl, it can't be that bad?" British walks backwards to Dani and wrap her arms around her as they continue to walk to the beach.

"I'm ok. It is just so heartbreaking when you really love a person you've been with for 3 years and they don't care about breaking your heart."

"Men gon' be men, and women tend to love harder than men. Trust me, you'll be ok. Men come and go. You have to let them know what they are missing out on."

"Easy for you to say." Dani mumbles as she rolls her eyes.

Nikki, British and Dani finally arrive to the beach and find a cool spot to chill. They see couples walking holding hands, people playing sand volleyball, people walking their dogs, and oh damn, sexy men! As we join them, British's attention instantly goes to the tall, light-skinned guy who is headed her way. "Oooh Shit! He's even finer with his shirt off." British can't help but smile as they both were standing in front of each other and started talking.

"Well! I brought sand to the beach, so my beach is better," he says.

"Oh Really?"

"Can I get some alone time with you tonight?"

"I don't see a problem with that."

"Good, meet me here tonight at sunset."

"Damn British! Who is this fine man right here?" Toya interrupts the conversation between the two.

"Uuuuhhhh, this is..."

"I'm Phil," he says as he reaches over British to shake Toya's hand.

"Yes, this is Phil. We met at the airport."

"Oh, this is the man you envisioned fucking..."

"So Phil, I will see you tonight!" British said as she pushes Toya away.

Phil laughs and gave British a kiss on the cheek as he walks away waving at the other girls.

After watching Phil walk away, we can't help but ask British what she has planned for them since she has the *sexing him* look all over her face.

"How do you know him, Brit?" Dani asks British as she slurps the last bit of drink she has in her cup.

"Oh, we just met yesterday at the airport. He is here with some of his frat brothers for a bachelor party," British said as she picked her drink up.

The sun is beaming on them where they are standing. We spot a bar on the beach and sit in the shade.

British opens her phone and sees that Jordan has called and texted her; "I guess you having some real fun?" Again, British don't even bother to respond to Jordan's text or return his call. This antisocial attitude she is having with Jordan comes directly from how things ended at their house before she left for the trip.

"Y'all! I am straight tripping how Jordan has been blowing my damn phone up since I have gotten here."

"Yea, we noticed how we haven't seen you engage in any conversations with his ugly ass."

"I'm good! I just want to enjoy my trip and not think about his ass at all. Especially since he thought it was cool to just leave the house and not even bother about giving me a proper goodbye."

"I feel you girl. Sometimes getting new ass will make you forget all about broke ass," Nikki laugh as she takes a shot.

We finish up at the bar and head back to our rental house. British gets ready for her night with Phil. Nikki gets ready for her play date with a guy she met at the beach bar. Toya and Sade cook for what they are considering Taco Night, and me and Dani take a swim in the private pool area of the rental home.

As British is heading to the agreed spot to meet Phil, she receives a text from Jordan saying he knows that she is on some fuck shit and better believe he is gon' show her he is not the one to be played with. British laughs and closes out of her Message App and continues her walk while enjoying the sand go between her toes.

"I've been waiting all day to see that pretty smile," Phil says as she approaches.

"Good! Because I've been waiting all day to give you this smile."

"I'm about to give you a night you will most definitely remember." Phil takes British hand and walks her down further. To her surprise, he has a beach picnic set up for the two of them. A nice red blanket is spread out on the sand, two wine glasses with wine already poured in them, and a plate full of fruit and cheese.

"I hope you like the idea," Phil says as he kisses British.

"I love it!" British replies with excitement.
As British and Phil lay across the blanket, they kiss. Phil sit up and unbuttons his shirt and raises up British's sundress. British closes her eyes and opens them quickly to make sure she is not dreaming again like she was on the plane. *"Yes!!! This is real,"* British say to herself as she and Phil make love.

The sound of the waves made the moment even more romantic. All British can do is enjoy the moment and wish it didn't have to end. She never thought in a million years that she would literally have sex on the beach. The good thing about the man she was giving her goodies to was that neither of them know one another. So if it comes out to be he is just looking for a fuck buddy while on this trip, British will be fine if she never sees Phil again.

****

The sun has risen, and it is time to say goodbye to Hawaii. Time sure goes by fast when you're having fun. We pack all our things and head to the airport. British is eager to get to the airport because she knows Phil will be there since his flight is also leaving. But unfortunately, they are on different flights this time. While we are on our way to the airport, British shares her experience and night with Phil with us. She says that for the first time she has not thought about Jordan and has not talked to him at all this entire trip. All of us are excited to hear it, but Dani is the only one asking why she feels like this if he is the person she's married to. British says that Jordan doesn't give her the attention that she is needing, and she has gotten more attention from Phil in just a few hours than she has gotten from Jordan in the 5 years they've been married.

Nikki interrupts and advises everyone that Jordan is a complete hoe and the best way to get even with a cheater is to be become a cheater. Dani continues to have her nonchalant look she has been having all weekend and is all in her phone not paying us any attention.

We arrived at the airport and complete the check-in process only for British to find out that Phil's flight has been delayed and is not leaving until later that night. British was hoping that Phil would still come to the airport so she could at least see him one last time.

****

British finally arrives home hoping Jordan would not be there. As she opens the garage, it is a complete disappointment to see that he IS. As British is getting her bags out of the car, she hears Jordan walking out of the garage door.

"How the fuck you get mad at me for being gone for 2 days and don't check in with you, but you gone for 7 days, and I don't receive any notifications from you?" Jordan angrily asks.

"How the fuck you married to a woman and instead of you giving her a proper goodbye and safe travels, you leave to go be with God knows who?" British laughingly says to Jordan as she gets her bags and walks around him.

"Oh, so this is a game to you? You don't want to play them games with me!"

"Goodnight Jordan."

As British gets into bed, all she can think about is Phil. Although she didn't get any contact information on him, she takes the experience with him as something she knew she was missing in her marriage. At this point, she knows it will soon be time to end her story with Jordan.

As morning comes, British wake up to the sound of the shower water running and Jordan on the phone whispering. She rolls over and realizes that she has a scheduled home showing and needs to send some paperwork to the client. She opens her Gmail account, and sees that Jordan's email is still signed in. Black Planet, eHarmony, Plenty of Fish, just to name a few. So many conversations from so many women, naked pictures, etc. This is the confirmation she needed to put his ass out. She slams her laptop closed and goes straight to the master bathroom where Jordan is taking a shit on the toilet. She is so mad that she doesn't even realize that he is straight funky. British just goes off.

"So, you enjoy looking at ugly naked bitches?"

"Huh? What are you talking about?"

"You know what the hell I'm talking about. Get your shit and get your nasty ass out my house!"

"Mane, you tripping!"

British goes to get her laptop and pulls up the emails to show Jordan since he is playing dumb. Even looking at the emails with his email address, this stupid nigga still denies it and keep saying he don't know where it come from.

"Just get the fuck out!" British says as she starts throwing his shit outside. Jordan really don't have much. He could pile all his little shoes and clothes up in his car.

British arrives to her home showing earlier than the scheduled time. She wants to have time to do her own walk-thru before the client comes so she will have everything in order. While standing in one of the upstairs windows, she notices a white BMW pull in the driveway. She starts her walk down the nice stairway of the home to see that her client is the same sexy bald-head guy she met at the bar the night before leaving for Hawaii.

"Hey Jayden! What are you doing here?" British asks as she stands in front of the door blushing.

"I want you to show me this house."

"Are you looking for a home or are you wasting my time?" She asks.

"I'm doing whatever it takes to see you," he replies.

She starts the showing upstairs since it was the closest to them. As British is pointing out all the features of the home, Jayden is checking out all the features British has. When they finish the upstairs, they go to view the downstairs.

"Here you have the open kitchen with the nice granite countertops, beautiful white tile on the floor, black cabinets..."

"And us on this counter," Jayden interrupts British as he lifts her on the countertop and begins kissing her.

British and Jayden had stayed behind after everyone left that night they met at the bar. He walked her to her car, and they talked for hours. They exchanged numbers and shared several calls and texts while she was away in Hawaii. There was strong chemistry between the two, however, British wasn't looking for anything serious. She just wanted to have some fun and get over Jordan's cheating ass.

British thought she was on top of the world. She had got sex on the beach and now sex in a house for sale. And as time went on, British and Jayden started hanging out more and developed a strong relationship. To British, he was everything she wanted in a man. To Jayden, she was someone he couldn't see his life without. He smelled good; he spoiled her; they took trips etc. What made their relationship perfect for them was that it was spontaneous! They did everything from having sex in the city park, the movie theatre, parking garages, you name it. According to them, this was something they both was missing from their previous relationships. These two became inseparable and the love for each other continued to grow. There was only one thing standing in the way -- they both had crappy relationships where they were lacking the spice. To them, it was time to end the past and start fresh with a future with each other.

Maya

Top of the morning! And as the sun started to beam in through my bedroom shades, I realize I didn't want to do a damn thing today. *"Let me get up and check the internet to see who done fucked up,"* I say to myself as I open my laptop and sign on to one of the hottest tabloid sites that always has all the updated tea. Then, my phone rings.

"Hello, this is Maya," I answer as I can hear someone breathing on the phone as if they are scared to announce themselves.

"Hello?"

"Yes, is this Maya Westbrook?" The caller finally said.

"Is this a bill collector?"

"Is this Maya?"

"Look, if you calling to ask for money, I don't know who she is and your number about to be on block."

"I am pregnant with Jordan Toliver's baby." The girl screams out and says.

"Yes, this is Maya, and you pregnant with whose baby?" I ask as I reach over to my nightstand and take out my recording device.

"Yes, I won't tell you my name, however, I know you are best friends with his wife. I have been trying to get in contact with him for months and he will not answer any of my calls," the girl says with an attitude. I knew if I gotten an attitude back with her, it was more than likely that the girl would eventually hang up and I would lose all access to this juicy information. Although I can't understand what her motive is by calling *me*, any news on Jordan is a plus for me. I asked the girl why she is reaching out to me to get in touch with Jordan. I let her know that I don't even like Jordan. I started to notice that the girl became quiet, and then I was interrupted with a reply.

"Look, I met Jordan while he was visiting Miami one weekend with his homeboys. We met at the club I was dancing at. He told me that he wanted to change my life. He reached in his pocket and pulled out a roll of money. As I was giving him a lap dance, he whispered in my ear and told me that I was leaving with him that night. Me -- not knowing who he really was, I seen dollar signs and knew he had money."

As this girl is trying to finish her story, I interrupt and state, "Girl, that bastard ain't got no money but carry on." She went on to say, "Well, he is getting it from somewhere. Every time he is in Miami, he buys me what I want, and he give me money on my bills. I told him that it was expensive to date me, and he told me he got me. When he came to Miami a month ago, I told him I was pregnant. He acted like he was cool with me telling him and told me that he was going to move me there with him so I wouldn't have to have the baby alone," all the while I'm recording everything she says on my recording device.

I blurt out and say, "You do know Jordan is married right and is living with his wife?" The girl goes on to say that Jordan never said he was married or single and he would come to Miami to make it all about them. As she continues to go on with the story, I texted Sade to see if she was home. It is so convenient for me and Sade to get together because we both live in the same apartment complex. Sade finally texts back and heads over.

Although I am recording the entire conversation, I can't wait until Sade gets here to just let her listen. Both of us just can't believe what we are hearing. So, the girl got done saying what she had to say, and I give her my reply.

"So, you mean to tell me you only saw this man whenever he came to Miami and you never, not once, thought to ask him if he was single? Then you got pregnant by a man that you don't even know? You don't know where he lives, what he does for a living, and if you will have his financial help with this child? So, let me ask you this... How are you so sure that this is Jordan's baby?" I made sure my recording device was close to the phone so I can have her answer loud and clear. Before the girl can even answer, I ask her how she knew to contact me and what is her name. The girl finally said her name is Monese. She says that after Jordan started ignoring all her calls and cut off all communication, she began to think back. She said that there was one weekend Jordan was there and they were at this restaurant in Miami called CHAR and Jordan ran into me there. So, as Monese is talking, I started to remember that when I was in Miami to cover a story, I *did* run into Jordan at CHAR. I asked her how she knew who I was, and she says that she had seen us when she came out of the bathroom, and when she asked him was I someone he knew, he just replied with no, just someone who wants to interview him. I start laughing. "Interview him? Who the hell is he to interview?" She tells me that she got my contact info because I left my card at the bar for the bartender, and when she stopped hearing from Jordan, the only thing she could think to do was to go back to the restaurant with hopes that the same bartender would be there and he still had my card.

When the conversation ended, Sade can't help but wonder what the hell are we going to do with this information. Although Sade hates Jordan, British is her friend, and she doesn't think I should put out something in the blogs that will destroy British or the friendship. I suggest that black mailing Jordan is the perfect answer.

"How will you blackmail him, girl?" Sade laughably asked me.

"You know British said that he won't sign the divorce papers. So, if we tell him that we are going to tell British about this girl if he don't sign, then he won't have no other choice," I say as I upload the recording to my laptop.

Although Sade is hearing what I am saying, she can't help but to wonder how all this will play out.

****

The same morning, as I walk into the office to start my day, I was stopped in my tracks by my nosey assistant, Ricky. "Dude what do you want already?" I say as I hand him my bags.

"Suuusss, we need to release some hot tea, or Bish, we gon' be fied," Ricky say to me as he threw my stuff to the side.

Everyone knows I am one of the hottest bloggers in the city and always release the juiciest tea. But for the last 2 months, I been slipping on my shit. I am one of the bloggers that my boss knows will keep the company in business. BOSSIP Ent is the hottest and largest blog firm here in the city. As I turn around in my chair, my boss enters through my office door.

"Miss lady, what the hell is your problem, and why haven't I gotten any hot releases?" My boss slams the day's newspaper on my desk.

"Do you see this? Do you see how our numbers are dropping and these other companies are releasing, and we are not?'

"I just haven't been able to put my finger on anything," I said as she slammed my laptop down.

"Well you better get me something within 30 days or you gon' be hearing about the tea instead of releasing it."

I know I must get some good tea and get some real good tea fast before I end up without a job. I fall back into my chair, and I start to think about this tea that I got this morning. I roll my eyes and buzzed for Ricky to come to my office.

"What, Bish?" Ricky says as he swings in the office with a nonchalant attitude.

"I am about to tell you something, and you better not mumble a word to anyone, or I am going to beat your ass myself," I say to Ricky as I get out of my seat to make sure no one is close by the door before I close it.

"Look, I got a phone call this morning that could change my career up in this Bish."

"Well do tell, because our career about to be saying paper or plastic," Ricky replied.

"Jordan has a baby on the way, and I got the proof on my laptop."

"Well what the hell you waiting on to release it?"

"If I release this, it will destroy British and probably our friendship."

"Fuck her! She probably don't really like your messy ass anyway. Bish, we got to release something fast, and unless you got some more juicy info, you need to come up off this proof." I heard everything Ricky was saying and knew he had a point. It's not the fact that I care about how Jordan will feel. It's all about British.

As I finish gathering my thoughts, I leave the office for the day to head to meet the girls as I do every Wednesday for Happy Hour, catch up on gossip, and spilling the tea at our favorite restaurant.

I got to the restaurant and so glad to see British has not gotten there yet, and Sade is already sitting. I run to the table so I can fill Sade in with what happened at work.

"Girl, don't you know that my boss came in today and told me that if I don't release anything in 30 days that my ass gon' be fired," I say as I take Sade's drink out her hand and drink the entire glass.

"Okay first, you owe me a drink. Second, you better get out there and find some tea," Sade said as she flags the waiter back to the table.

"Sade, I have some tea," I said.

"What tea?" She asked. Then I told her about the baby on the way.

"Look, I know what you are thinking, but damn girl, I got to pay the bills," I said.

"So, you will actually risk your friendship with your high school best friend to release a messy story for the world to see and destroy someone you say you love?"

"Okay, so is British going to take care of me?" I asked.

"Well here she come, so why don't you ask her!"

I almost choked when I notice British was walking to the table.

"Hey Chica's!" British said to me and Sade as she gave each of us a hug.

"Hey Girl!" Sade says as she gives me the side eye.

I hesitated as I slowly spoke and hugged British. British sat down and looked at the menu. I looked at British and told her that I needed her honest opinion on something. As British put down the menu to give me her undivided attention, I start saying....

"So, I have this friend who job is on the line and her boss has told her that if she doesn't improve in her job performance in 30 days, she is going to be jobless. She does good at what she does but the only reason why she is unable to give her boss this change in performance is because it involves someone very close to her. Her boss doesn't care. However, if she loses her job then she will be on the streets because she wouldn't have any other income to make sure her bills are paid. What do you think she should do?"

British bucks her eyes, takes a drink and says, "Well Bish, you probably should do what is best for you and think about what is more important, and before you ask me how I know it's you, your ass has never been able to lie."

We continue our gossip as any other time and say our goodbyes as we leave the bar. Me and Sade leave together, and the ride home is kind of silent. As Sade turns the radio down, she asked me what I am going to do about the news. I mumble and tell her I don't know, but I'm going to pray about it while I go home and add my bills up.

When we get out my truck and get ready to go into our apartment complex, we run right into Jordan.

"Well I'll be damned! They say when you speak of the devil they show up," I say as I give Jordan a smirk.

"Hey Sade," Jordan says as he gives her a hug.

"So, Jordan, it looks like you will be the talk of the town in just a few," I say patting Jordan on his back.

"What the hell are you talking about with your thirsty ass," Jordan asks me as he pushes my hand off him. Jordan and I can't stand each other, and it is no secret. British and I were college roommates, and I always make sure that every time I seen Jordan, I will throw up in his face how British would be better off with her ex Damien.

I couldn't wait to tell Jordan that I know about his affair with Monese and that he has a baby on the way. And I will tell British if he doesn't give her the divorce she wants so she can move on with her life. Of course, Jordan gives me the look like he don't know what I am talking about and says he doesn't care what I tell British. He left to go get in his bright yellow Camaro and drove away. Jordan always kept a nonchalant attitude which irks the hell out of everybody.

I realize that we are at our apartment complex and I wonder why the hell Jordan is leaving from it. "Girl who is he fucking in this building," I say laughing as Sade and I get on the elevator. It was good that we stayed on the same floor because we could get together when it was needed. We get off the elevator, say our good nights and head to our apartments. After I open my front door and closed it, all I can do is just lean up against it and slide down and go into deep thought. "What the hell am I going to do?" I thought to myself. I got up and threw my jacket and purse on the futon in the sunroom of my studio apartment. I can't help but to pour me a glass of wine and damn near cry.

****

Another morning at the office and another morning with no tea to spill. As I sit in my office, I start to have a strange feeling that my boss is on her raggedy ass way. Sure as shit, she walks in.

"Good Morning, what you got for me?" She asks standing in the doorway popping her knuckles.

I blow and say, "Unfortunately, I don't have anything. However, I may have something, but I am still working on the details to make sure it is credible to use."

"Who does it involve?"

"Well let's just say, it is someone real close to this city."

"Well time is ticking so hurry up and get this story together, finished and on the blog."

"Yes Ma'am," I say as I just sink down in my chair. While I'm opening my desk drawer to get some Excedrin to take for the headache I was starting to have,

Ricky walks in and just slams the door and stretches across my desk.

"Bish, we gon' be fied fied," Ricky said.

"Something has to come up soon," I replied opening my folder on my computer that contains all my gossip, including the one about Jordan.

Ricky goes on to say that friends fall out all the time, so unless I am going to move in with British, then I need to be releasing this story so we can continue to eat. All Ricky cares about is the fact that we will be getting a real large bonus if we release the story. I tell Ricky that real friends don't intentionally hurt friends and that I really don't think that losing my friendship with someone that I have been friends with since high school is worth it.

Both Ricky and I begin gathering our things, I tell Ricky that I was going to take some time and have a private conversation with British. It was only right. I left and got in my truck and reached for my phone to send British a text.

"Hey B, we need to get together over drinks -- have something I need to speak with you about."

I got ready to lay my phone down and notice British had replied so quickly.

"Is the B for Bitch or British? Lol!" I can't help but laugh and hope that British keeps that same energy when we talk.

British and I got to the restaurant at the same time. As we are sitting, I become hesitant about giving British a hug.

"So, what has been going on with you?" I say just to start up a conversation.

"Girl nothing. Just showing houses and showing love to the man that I have found." British replies.
I know that British has started a new relationship which I hope that when I break this news, she will say that she doesn't care because she is over Jordan. British has a smile on her face that I have never even seen before, which kind of give me a little of hope.

"Ok, so this is the reason why I brought you here. A few weeks ago, I received a phone call from this girl who is a stripper in Miami. She advised me that she was pregnant, and she wanted to call and make me aware of it. She also told me that she met Jordan at the strip club she works at and she went back to the hotel with him where they had sex. Since that day, they had been in a relationship. He would send her money, take her shopping and spend a lot of time with her every time he was in the city. She broke the news to Jordan that she was pregnant, and she has not heard from him since. When trying to locate him, she found out that he was married and that he did not live in New Orleans like he told her."

As I am trying to finish the story, British cuts me off. "So you are telling me that Jordan's trips to Miami was because he had a Bitch there and now she is claiming to be pregnant by him? Girl this some bullshit that I don't even care to entertain."

I can see the hurt in British's eyes although she's really trying to be strong and act like she really doesn't care. At this point, I am regretting I even said anything to her.

"Maya, why did you feel the need to bring me to a restaurant to tell me this rather than telling me over the phone and better yet, not telling me when the broad

even called you?" British asks me as I am trying to find the right words to say. Right now, I can't do anything but be silent and accept every attitude British is giving me. I even think it's probably not a good idea to say anything about releasing the story or wondering if she would even care that I will possibly lose my job if I don't release the story. I am confused as fuck. Just as I am thinking, my phone rings. When I looked at the number, I realized that the number looked familiar but was not completely sure where I had seen the number.
"Hello?" I answered.

"Hello Ms. Maya, this is Monese. The girl who is pregnant by Jordan. I need to speak with you about something." Mane, I bucked my eyes and couldn't help but look at British. It was all over her face that she could hear the conversation. British snatches the phone from my ear.

"Hello, this is British. Can I help you?"

"Well, well, well!!! Hello Mrs. Toliver. I see Maya has spilled the beans on my pregnancy. British paused and then begin to let them words sink in her head. She can't help but look at me with such disappointment.

Dani

What it feels like to have a broken heart... Dani takes a moment as she starts to write in her journal the things she wants her heart breaker to know but can never find the courage to say.

"Let me explain to you what it feels like to be told you are perfect, and you will always be taken care of. Let me convey the emotions that rip through the heart of someone when she is convinced that she is someone's forever. Let me express the hope and loyalty that is instilled in a woman who built up numerous walls only to feel as it was OK to let them down for the man who pulled her deeply in love with him. I cannot formulate those emotions into words, and I cannot describe the way it felt to have you tear my heart into pieces.

I want you to know that I loved you. I loved you through every emotional part of the roller coaster you brought into my life. I loved you on the days you made me feel special and the days you left me feeling all alone. I loved you through changing circumstances and the rapid movement of time. I even loved you when you decided to make me feel like you didn't love me anymore. But what I want you to get out of this letter mostly is that I still love myself and I still know what love really is.

The difference between you and I is that my love is unwavering. It is a love that is deep inside of my soul. It is a love that was taught to me as a child -- that people will hurt me time after time. You have shattered my heart, but you have not shattered my love. Because love is not something that is cast aside and broken. It is something that resides safely inside of me, and it has a tool for forgiveness and strength. Love is faith when we lose it in humanity, and it is being able to see my own beauty and potential even when you have made these things feel non-existent. Love is a perpetual joy that has saved me when all hope felt lost. So, love is not something you can take from me.

You have broken my heart, but you have not broken my love. I know you have love deep inside of you as well, and I know my love allows me to genuinely hope that you will understand it one day. There is no simple letter written about a simple heartbreak, but there is one simple concept, and that is that love is the most powerful entity in the world. So, I am going to allow a few more tears to fall right now in your honor. I will most likely shed more when I listen to songs you created on a playlist just for us or see something that reminds me of when you made me smile. But I will be OK. I will be OK because the love inside of me is strong and true. I will also be OK because no matter how many times a person tramples on my heart, they will never take my love. No one can, not even you.

With love,

The one whose heart you broke!!!

Dani reads the letter she wrote over and over, trying to build up enough courage to tell him exactly what she had written in her journal.

"I just want him to understand that he broke my heart and he needs to know that it is not okay," Dani says while leaning her head back on her chair. Dani have been in this relationship with this mystery man for over 3 years on and off, and she has never brought him around her friends because she didn't want anyone to judge her. While Dani is sitting on her gray chase lounge trying to decide on the delivery of this message, she receives a text from her heart breaker. She would always fight herself with really letting this man go, because she knows that he is not good for her, but it is a struggle because of the love that she has for this man.

"What's up?" She replies to his message.

"You!"

"Here you go. I told you to stop texting me. If you can't give me what I want, then there is no need for us to continue this roller coaster of a relationship that we have."

"Look mane, I am about to come over there so we can talk."

"UUUUHHHHH!!!! Why can't I just say no and let this man go on about his business?" Dani would always ask herself this one question that she seemed to not be able to find the answer to. She wants to talk to someone so bad because she feels so alone, but who can she talk to? She can't go to her friends because she knows that neither of them will understand why she is in this relationship, and they will only judge her. So, she is always left with leaving her frustrations balled up on the inside just building up more and more.

"Hey Bae!" He exclaims.

"What do you want? You get on my damn nerves."

"Yo body don't say that when I'm all up in it."

"You get on my nerves," Dani says as she is trying to resist him kissing her from her forehead to her ears to her lips. All she can really think about was the fact that she knew deep down inside that she really loves this man.

As always, they start their time together with sex. One reason why Dani is so in love is because the sex is so damn good. Actually, it's the best sex she has had in any man she has been with. Looking up at her vaulted ceilings, Dani forgot all about the thoughts of needing to give him this long ass letter she had written to him. But of course, he makes her forget anything that deals with leaving him.

"Aite baby! I got to get home. I will text and check on you in a little while." She always hated the time when they had to say goodbye to each other because they would have so much fun together.

Dani works as a licensed counselor in her city. She is always voted the best and she always come highly recommended. She is great at what she does. As any day in the office, she gets ready for her daily appointments. She goes over the profile sheets of every person she is seeing, and one person's profile sticks out to her. A man who is cheating on his wife and doesn't know how to stop. "How can I counsel this man?" Dani thinks to herself as she throws her pen down and lets out a big sigh.

"Good Afternoon! Your 3 o'clock is ready for you," Dani's assistant says as she peaks her head in the door.

"Hello, I'm Dani. Nice to meet you," Dani says as she shakes her first client's hand and leads him to where he can sit.

"So, let's start with you telling me a little about yourself."

"My name is Frank, and I just need help with figuring out why my wife isn't enough for me to stop cheating."

"So, are you saying you are lacking some things in your marriage that you are finding in other women?"

"Absolutely! However, I love my wife, but I just can't stop cheating." Dani just paused for a minute and her mind began wondering. "What in the world can I say to this man? How can I tell him what he needs to start and stop doing? Should I even tell him?"

These were the questions Dani keep replaying back in her head while she pretends that she was writing notes when she is really writing "WTF" throughout the page.

"What are you lacking from your marriage that you are getting from cheating?" She asked him.

"Well me and my wife have been together for a while. We went to high school together and started dating after high school. We got married, and it is like she feels like since we have been together for a long time and have history, then that is enough for us."

"WOW!" Dani continues to listen to the counseling session and counts down the time left.

The session ends, and Dani shows Mr. Frank to the door with hopes of him not wanting to come back.

"How do I set up my next appointment?" Frank asks as he is walking out the door.

"Shit!" Dani thinks to herself. "My secretary will be able to assist you with that. However, I think I am completely booked for the next 2 months, but she can check for you." Dani gives her secretary a look like, "Don't book this fool another appointment."

She tries to hurry up at the office so she can leave and not be late meeting us. Although she really is not in the mood to hear any gossip, she needs the drink badly. She leaves and walks down the halls of her office in her space grey business suit with her Coach briefcase. She has the walk and look of success. She has a reputation that she has worked hard to get and doesn't want anything to stand in the way of it changing.

Dani arrives to the restaurant in her white Land Rover and pulls to the door so the valet attendant can take and park her truck. She finds Nikki and Toya sitting in a section on the restaurant's patio.

"Hey ladies," Dani says as she goes around the table to hug both girls.

"Okay, Bish!" Nikki says as she is checking out Dani in her bad suit.

"So, what are you ladies chatting about?"
"The usual! Jordan and British. British and this new guy she been talking to these past few months..."

"New guy? Dani interrupts Nikki almost about to choke on her salad she had just started eating which was already on the table.

Nikki and Toya give Dani the look of *where you been*? So, turns out British and Jayden has been spending a lot of time together. No one has quite met him yet, but the way British has been these past few months, it seems as if she has gotten her happiness back.

Now as for Jordan, we really don't even care to know what he has been up to since British rarely even brings his name up. British has been on cloud nine knowing that no one really has all the details of their relationship as of now. All we know is, they are living that life.

"So, Dani, how are things going with you and your relationship?" Toya takes a sip of her drink awaiting a reply. Dani takes a moment to look at the sky and feels herself about to cry.

"Y'all just wouldn't understand." She really wants to get her things and just leave because she hates it when someone asks her about anything that is going on in the relationship that has her heart broken.

"Hey, Bishes!" British walks in and gives everyone at the table a hug.

"Oh, we were just talking about you. We didn't think you would come since your new boo been keeping you away from us," Toya say to British as she give her a hug.

"Girl, where has this man been all my life?"

"So, you and Jordan are not together anymore?" Dani can't wait until British finishes yapping so she can answer the question.

"Jordan who? Hunny, ain't nobody thinking about that cheater. Hell, I wish he would stop calling me."

"Oh, I didn't know you two had broken up. Sorry to hear that."

"No need, Dani. I mean you are the only one that feels like that anyway." We all laugh.

So, it is no secret that everyone wants to know what has been going on with British and this new guy. She goes on to tell us how she has fallen completely in love with this man and has officially filed for a divorce from Jordan. We are shocked to learn that Jordan is not cooperating and don't want to sign the divorce papers when he is the one who has done all the cheating. Typical man. She even shares how a girl had called her from Jordan's phone to let her know that she is in a relationship with Jordan and that they will soon be moving in together because she is pregnant.

"Girl what? Dani yells out.

"Yes ma'am! I mean the day I put him out I logged onto my computer and seen that he had been having conversations with all these women on these dating sites and been sending naked pictures back and forth."

"And why won't he give you a divorce?"

"Who knows. But we all know that Jordan is nothing without me, so he supposed to be staying with some woman. But I don't really give one flying fuck, as long as he is not in my house anymore."

"That's interesting." Dani has this confused look on her face but keep on sipping her drink.

As we are finishing up with our food and drinks, British can't help but notice a familiar face at the bar.

She wants to play the 'I got to go to the bathroom' game in order to see if the person at the bar is who she thinks it is. Instead, she just gets up and goes because she is too old to play them games.

"B, are you gone?" Nikki asks British as she is walking away.

"No, I will be right back, she says holding up her finger. Just as British is heading to the bar, she is stopped in her tracks by Jordan.

"Hey, we need to talk." Jordan says as he grabs British by her arm.

"What the hell do you want?"

"Why you ain't been answering my calls?"

"First off, don't touch me. Second, get the hell out of my face. Third, what the hell do you want?" As British is trying her best to get away from Jordan, the girls start to walk up behind her and ask if there is a problem.

"Mane, I'm trying to talk to my wife," Jordan says as he stands in front of Nikki.

"She not your wife anymore," Nikki says as she laughs in Jordan's face. He tries his best to get British away from us so he can talk to her.

"You see she don't want to talk to you Jordan. She got to get to her man." Dani says to Jordan as everybody turns around and look at her with the *WHAT THE FUCK* look.

Jordan turns around so fast with the look in his eyes of wanting to smack the hell out of Dani.

"What mother fucking man?" Jordan say as he looks back at British.

British smiles at Jordan and while she slowly leans over to his ear, she whispers, "Nigga you wanted a stripper remember?"

****

Dani finally made it home. As she opens the door to her beautifully decorated condo and to the smell of the pound cake fragrance, all she can think about is why her heart will not let go of a man who actions show that he doesn't love her.

She is taking off her shoes and clothes to prepare for her shower, and she hears her door opening.

"Turn your key in please," Dani says as she rolls her eyes but was kind of glad the bastard decided to give her some of his time.

Dani continues removing her clothes and gets in the shower where she knows he will soon join her. All she wants is some good sex. As always, she knows that every time she is mad, he will try to change that attitude by eating her out. She giggles to herself as she begins washing her body with her dove soap. Sex in the shower was always a win.

Dani always forgets about anything this man has done when they have sex which is probably the problem and probably the reason why she just can't leave him alone. To him, he feels like having sex will make all the issues go away but to Dani, it only sweeps the issues under the rug. All she knows is that she really loves this man and really doesn't see herself being with anyone else.

After the sex, Dani decides she wants to get some things off her mind and feel like a talk is needed. "Baby we need to talk." Dani raise up as she kisses him on his cheek.

"Aw hell, what did I do now baby?" Dani's lover asks.

"Why do you have to have done something?" Dani asks as she raises up to talk.

She is really struggling with the therapy session she had with her patient, and she wants to share it to get some advice. However, she is hoping that he will be able to help her out to help her client. Dani starts to say that she had a client who wanted to know why he keeps cheating and needing to know why his wife wasn't enough for him to only want to be with her and not another woman. Although she tells him she need some advice, what she really wants to know is what will his answer be.

They begin talking about the issue, and then it is time for him to put on his clothes and leave for the night. These are the moments that Dani hates the most. Although she knew what she was getting herself into, she just can never really understand why they are still in the same boat as they were when they first started their relationship.

As the sun shined into the curtains of Dani's wide windows, she rolled over to the sound of a text message alert. "Good Morning! You ready to let me take you out now?" The text message read.

A few weeks earlier while Dani was leaving the parking garage of her office, she ran into this tall, yellow, sexy body, handsome man who also worked in the same building. He immediately caught her attention. As they exchanged numbers, she started to wonder if it was a good idea to start something new with a whole different person while she is still trying to figure out what she has going on with the man she has been with for several years. Or should she just not entertain the thought at all. Although her heart is with the man she has shared and built so much with, she can't help but realize that the same man hasn't even busted a grape to deliver all the things and plans that he had promised.

"Good Morning, how are you this morning?" Dani asked.

"I would be better if I can see you again over a nice dinner." As Dani read that message over and over, she leaned back on her sofa and thought *fuck it!*

66

She replied to the message and advised the charming guy that she would be open to going out. Then, she showers and gets ready to just lounge for the day. As she lay on her silk pillowcases a small smile starts to come across her face. She is kind of excited about the date that had just been set up and is kind of looking forward to it.

****

"You look beautiful," Kendall said to Dani as she sits down in the chair that he has pulled out for her. She stared at him as he continued to compliment her. She can't help but to wish that she was staring at the man she is so in love with.

As Dani continues with her date, she had a jaw dropping moment. "What the fuck?" Dani says out loud. Before Kendall can even ask her what is wrong, she had already gotten up from her seat.

"Hey Jordan! Who is this? Dani say with an attitude as she looks in the eyes of the woman who is sitting next to Jordan.

As Jordan is getting ready to answer, Kendall approaches Dani to ask her if she is ok. He take her by her hand and kind of gets close to her as he holds out his other hand to introduce himself to Jordan and the lady.

"Mane who the hell is you?" Jordan asks as he stands up in front of Kendall.

"This is my friend Kendall. Now, who is this bitch?" Dani asks rudely. At this very moment, Kendall knows it is more than just seeing a friend out, so he thinks it is best to just end the night early.

They say their goodbyes and Dani tells Kendall she will see him later.

Dani walks into her apartment to find Jordan sitting on her couch. She is so furious at Jordan that she really is not up for his bullshit. That's right. Jordan is Dani's secret lover that no one knows about! Of course, this is a secret that must be kept because Jordan is her best friend's husband. They know it is wrong to be together, but they have a bond that no one will ever understand. The love they share for each other is unexplainable.

"So, you going on dates and shit?"

"I'm going on what you were on."

"That was my homegirl from high school."

"Well the bitch didn't look too homie to me."

Jordan and Dani go back and forth for hours until he gets a phone call that he must step out and take. When Jordan comes back in, he tells Dani that he has to go and will just see her later. Of course, he has an attitude, so he just leaves and slams the door behind him without even saying bye. It is something he does every time him and Dani are at odds.

After only a few minutes have passed by, Dani picks up her phone and calls Jordan. They go on and on for several minutes. Jordan expresses how she shouldn't be talking to anyone else and Dani expresses how she gets so sick of Jordan thinking he can just do what he wants but when she pull a *him* on him, he gets mad and feel as if she is disrespecting him and their relationship.

"Aite mane, I'm pulling up at the house so I will holla at you later," Jordan says before hanging up in Dani's face.

She is so tired of being frustrated with Jordan's shit. She is tired of not being able to have the relationship that she really wants because he is married. She knows what she wants, but of course her heart and the love she has for Jordan is what constantly holds her back from being in a real relationship.

Dani sat in the middle of her bed and just thought about Kendall and how much of a gentleman he was. She wants to call him, but she is unsure if he is even still interested in her after the big blow up that happened while they were on their date. Just as she is thinking, her phone ring. To her surprise, it is Kendall.

"Hello!" Dani say as she is trying not to sound as if she's excited to hear his voice.

"Hey love, I wanted to make sure you are ok. I didn't hear back from you."

"Yes, I am okay! I first want to apologize about what happened."

"You're good. I understand how things can be when you see an ex." Dani bucked her eyes while holding her head back because she knows that this man is not an ex but the one who holds her heart. Kendall lets Dani know that he wants to see her again but only if she is up to it. Dani take a long breath and say, "Sure, I would love that. I am free now if you want to meet." Kendall informs Dani that she can come to his house if she feels comfortable, and they can sit back and chill. Dani is up for it and tell him to send her the address and she will be on her way.

She arrives to what seem to be a very nice neighborhood. Nice houses, clean yards, quiet area. Dani continues to follow her GPS and she finally pulls in Kendall's driveway. He has already texted Dani to tell her that he's in the shower and gives her instructions on how to access her way into the garage. She walks into his home and instantly is amazed. Not surprising that he has a nice home because he drives a nice car and carries himself nicely. Dani sits on the nice beige sectional that is in his living room while she waits for him to get out of the shower. Minutes goes by and she hears the sexy sound of Kendall's voice.

"Hey, what's going on?" Dani turned around and couldn't help but watch this tall, sexy, banana colored man walk in front of her and sit next to her.

Kendall pours them a glass of wine and ask what type of movies she likes. As they sip on wine attempting to watch a movie, Dani can't help but to think about how this is what she wants for her life – to be with a man who she can come home to, chat about her day, sip on wine and have movie nights. She realized that she hasn't had this type of life in over 4 years because she is just into a man who cannot offer that. So, for the first time in years, Dani can't help but enjoy every moment with the man who is not the one who is hurting her.

Hours go by and it is getting late. Dani and Kendall have spent hours talking and lost track of time. Although Kendall does not want her to leave, Dani knows it's best to just end the night and go home. She checks her phone and it's no surprise that she doesn't have not one missed call or text from Jordan. "I guess that is what happens when you are messing with a married man!" Dani thinks to herself as she put her phone down and started driving out of Kendall's driveway.

On the ride home, she constantly asks herself if she should really move on. She knows that being with Jordan is not the right thing to do because not only is he married, but he is also married to her best friend. She knows deep down in her heart that although they share so much love for each other, they will never be with each other.

Dani starts to picture the night that she had with Kendall and compared it to the nights she has had with Jordan. When she is with Jordan, they are always cooped up in the house. Although he gives her the best sex and shows her so much attention, they can't ever leave the house and have an ordinary date night. With Kendall, they have been on dates, spent time together at his home, and were making plans to take a trip, because Dani kept stressing to him repeatedly that she needs a vacation. She keeps saying to herself that it really should not be this hard to decide which man she should be with. But her heart just keeps making the wrong decision...

By the time she had pulled up at home, Kendall was calling her phone to make sure she made it home.

"Hello?" Dani answers as she is getting her things to get out the car and go in the house.

"Hey, just wanted to make sure you had made it home okay," Kendall says to Dani.

"Yea, I am walking in the house now. Thanks for checking."

"Of course! I hope you enjoyed tonight and thinking about getting out again. I got season passes to my college basketball games. I would love for you to go with me tomorrow night if you are free."

"Sure!" Dani says as she finally gets into the house and throws her stuff down on the couch. She is kind of excited about the attention she is getting from Kendall and the fact that she can finally get a chance to get out of the house, arm and arm with someone she likes. She has not been on a real date in 4 years because, of course she and Jordan can't be seen in public.

Over a month's time, Dani and Kendall start hanging out more and more, and she starts to forget about Jordan's trifling ass. Every time she speaks with him, all he wants to do is argue because he knows that Dani has started seeing someone, and he is not able to keep tabs on her like he had been doing for the past few years.

One night as Dani was sleeping, she is awakened with what seemed to be a stomach bug. She jumped up and realized that she had to throw up and can barely hold it in before making it to the toilet.

"OMG! Where did this come from?" She thinks to herself. She finishes cleaning herself up and has this strange feeling about possibly being pregnant. Although she does not want that to be true, she can't help but to think about it because she was already late on her period. She leaves out of the bathroom and sits on the floor beside her bed. She picks up her phone and sends me a text.

"Hey sis! WYD?" It was taking me awhile to text back. Dani knew she needed to tell someone, and she do not want to trust anyone other than her sister.

"Hey Sis, I am headed home. What's up?" I respond. While reading the reply I sent her, Dani tells me that she needs to talk to me and slides in that she thinks she is pregnant. So, of course Dani knows that if she doesn't add any tea in the text, I won't be bothered and can care less.

"Oh wait! Okay, Bish, let me whip this thang around. Here I come," I text back. Twenty minutes have passed, and my ass is knocking on Dani's door.

"Okay, so what are you talking about, you think you could be pregnant? I just know you haven't gotten yourself into some shit you can't get out of," I say as I enter through Dani doors handing her a pregnancy test.,

"Wait, why did you bring a test?" Dani asked me.

"We need to find out today if you are pregnant so you can call that bastard and tell him what he needs to be doing," I tell her as I escort her to the bathroom to make sure she peas on the stick.

Dani takes the test and just as she thought, she is pregnant. She just starts to cry.

"Okay, okay! It is not the end of the world. You just need to get up and get yourself together," I tell Dani. She just looks up at me and replied, "Sis, you just don't understand. I have really fucked up bad."

At this point, I know something is wrong with Dani. I have been her sister all my life, so I can pretty much tell when something is really bothering her. Dani knows it is time to talk to me about the affair that she is having.

"Sis, you gon' need to sit down for this one," Dani says to me as we both sit on the couch. With tears in her eyes, Dani comes out and tells me that not only is she pregnant by a married man, but that married man is Jordan.

"Bish, what!" I say as I try my best not to slap the shit out of Dani. "What the hell you mean you are pregnant by Jordan? Jordan the fuck who? I know you not talking about your best friend's husband Jordan. Really Dani? How stupid and desperate can you be?" I go on and on until I start to get cotton mouth. I can tell that I am hurting her feelings, but right now, all I can think about is how Jordan is manipulating my sister into thinking that it is cool to do this.

"How could you destroy and come between a happy home? Let alone the home of your best friend. Then out of all the married men, you choose Jordan cheating, dumb ass," I say rolling my eyes.

Dani raised up and said, "Just because a man cheats, does not mean that they are a bad person. Some of them are just unhappy in their marriage and they'd rather cheat than walk away. Everyone always walks around and speaks on marriage like it is all that. Being married does not mean you are satisfied emotionally and physically. And it damn sure don't mean that you are getting your needs met. It only means that you are legally bound to someone that you may or may not love anymore. So, some married people seek to find those things in other people."

I just looked at Dani in pure disgust and say, "Bitch, I used to think that you were the best and smartest counselor around, but now I am convinced that you are just as stupid as the ones who agree with that bullshit you just said. I sure in the hell hope you are not feeding women this bull. You say that men are looking for happiness and trying to find the love that they don't get at home. My question is this... if they are cheating looking for that, then why you women only end up with the penis? Hell, if that's the case, you might as well go surf the web and purchase one."

Both my sister and I went back and forth for hours until I told her that if she doesn't tell British what she has been doing, then I am going to be forced to do it. Dani know the right thing to do is to come clean, but she also knows that British was her best friend and her friendship will in fact be over. But what scares Dani the most about telling British is that she knows British is crazy as hell.

Sade

"Do you know what today is? It's our Anniversary!!!" Chad sings the words out loudly as he walks into his and Sade's bedroom filled with balloons, gifts, and breakfast for two. June 4, 2016 is a day they first met, and now they are celebrating their 4th year.

"Oh Baby, you always know how to make me smile," Sade says as she leans over to give Chad a kiss. Chad smiles as he and Sade finish opening the gifts they have for each other.

As Sade is getting ready to head out, I call her.

"Hey Girl!"

"So, girl, can you pick me up from the dealership this evening? I need to drop my car off for maintenance, I said.

"Got some gas money?"

"Naw, Bish that's why I am calling you instead of calling Uber," I replied.

"Girl you know I got you," Sade laughs as she hangs up the phone with me so she could rush out the door.

Sade is in her last year of nursing school and can't wait to start her dream career and marry her high school sweetheart, Chad. He proposed to Sade after two years of dating. Although it is a dream to marry Chad, Sade keeps putting the wedding off because she is scared she is going to go through the issues her friends have. Chad, who has his own barber shop and who is also best friends with Jordan, does not pressure Sade into marrying him any sooner than she wants to.

It's a busy Saturday morning at the shop so Chad heads in early. With a shop full of clients, shop talk begins. Chad has the hottest barbershop in the city. Although it is a barbershop, it is the man cave that men have away from home. There is a bar, a pool table, game room, massage parlor and everything else you can think of.

"Dude, I need to get a massage from that fine ass gal," Jordan says to Chad as he walks in the shop and right past everyone.

"Hello Mr. Jordan! Are you ready for your appointment?" Kenya says as she bites on her finger while Jordan comes in and starts to take his clothes off.

"Would you like for me to step out while you get ready?" Kenya asks.

"Why? I thought you would rather enjoy the show," Jordan says flirtatiously. As Jordan continues to take off his clothes, Kenya watches him walk over to her massage table, naked with the towel in his hand rather than wrapping it around him.

Kenya is a licensed massage therapist who has this nice body and catches everyone's eye. She is Chad's first cousin who started working in his shop right after she finished school.

"Oohh Baby, that feels so good!" Jordan say as he slowly takes Kenya's hands and places her finger in his mouth. Kenya smiles as Jordan slowly pulls her on top of him while he sits up on the table and kisses her all over her body. He gets up and tells her to lay down and let him give her a massage. Jordan takes the massage oil that is sitting on the table beside the bed and firmly rubs it over her body while he kisses every inch. He flips her on her back and begins eating her out. He knows the way he eats a woman drives them crazy and once he is finish, he has them where he needs them to be--ready to fuck.

After the appointment, Jordan walks out of the room towards the lobby while Kenya follows fixing her clothes. Jordan can't help but see Sade looking at him with pure anger in her eyes. Of course, he figures she know what happened but, in a way, he doesn't give damn and speaks to her anyway.

Sade turns to Chad and tells him that Kenya needs to find somewhere else to hoe around, because they didn't build this establishment to become a hoe house.

"Babe, that is my cousin, and I told her mom I would take care of her," Chad say whispering to Sade.

"I don't give a damn!" Sade says loudly as everyone turns and look at her.

Chad can see Kenya walking towards them so he tells Sade they will have a discussion when he gets home.

"Hey Sade, is there a problem?" Kenya asks Sade with a fake smile. Sade rolls her eyes as she turns to the direction the sound is coming from.

"Bitch do you pay any bills here? Do you make any decisions around here?" Sade asks.

"If you have a problem with me then you need to address it because whether you want me here not, I am staying because this is my cousin's shop, and you can't make me leave." Kenya throws her hair to the back.

Sade laughs, looks at Chad and said, "Baby, you better let this trick know who the hell I am." Then she turns to Kenya, "No better yet, I will let you know that I am the HBIC- THE HEAD BITCH IN CHARGE. My name is on this building and I make the rules." Sade grabs her purse to leave because she saw herself slapping the hell out of Kenya.

****

2:00 p.m. has arrived and Sade is so excited to be meeting her girls at the bridal boutique to look at wedding dresses. Sade and Chad have been engaged for a few months, but they have never set an official wedding date. Chad always asks Sade about it but never put any pressure on her. She always says she is kind of scared to get married because she has seen so much going on in her BFF's marriage.

"Hello, my name is Sade, and I have a 2 p.m. appointment," she says to the receptionist. As the receptionist shows Sade to the back, the other girls arrive.

"Hey Bride-to-be," the girls say to Sade as they each go over to hug her. The receptionist places the girls in the back and tells them that someone will be with them shortly, but they can go ahead and start looking and pulling dress ideas from the rack to try on.

"Y'all not gon' believe what happened this morning at the shop!" Sade says.

"Girl what?" Nikki asks as she is looking through the racks.

"So, I stop by the shop this morning to take Chad some breakfast, and his cousin almost got her ass beat."

Nikki stop in her tracks, "Wait, the cousin that is a hoe?"

"Yes, that bish." Sade roll her eyes. "So, I'm standing next to Chad, right? I see Jordan come from the back then Kenya brings her ass out." She is not realizing what she is saying because she is mad and just trying to get the story out. British stops what she is doing.

"Jordan?" she asks.

Sade realizes what she said, and she tries to go on with the story and not mention that she is sure they had sex.

"Yes, so me and Chad are going back and forth, and she walks up and asked if there was a problem? I had to really calm by nerves." Sade goes on with the story of how Kenya told her that Chad is her cousin and that Sade cannot put her out. As Sade is trying to finish telling us about what happened, Dani interrupts and ask, "Are you saying that Jordan and Kenya were together in the back?"

While everyone looks at Dani, Dani looks at British and says, "I am saving you the trouble of asking, Hunny."

British laughs, "Girl, I don't give a damn who Jordan sticks his thing up in. He gon' end up catching other babies and STDs at the rate he is going."

While we were shopping and kicking it, Nikki can't help but to notice how funny Dani is looking after Sade broke the news about Jordan and Kenya at the barbershop. She hangs the dress she had in her hand back on the rack and pulls Dani to the side and says, "Bish, if I didn't know any better, I would think you have a thing for Jordan!"

Dani look all puzzled and replies, "Why would you think that? I don't want Jordan cheating ass and besides, British is my best friend," Dani frowns at Nikki and rushes off.

"Uh huh, Bish," Nikki say laughing and walks in the other direction.

As we are finishing up and getting our things, Nikki blurts out, "Ok! So, are we ready to hit the spot now because I need a damn drink?" Nikki is always the one who is ready for a drink and ready to party. "It's time to celebrate Sade's ass! So, come on let's go," Nikki says as she dances her way out of the door.

Everyone walks out to leave and head our way to the hang out spot. Of course, Sade is trailing me because I have to drop off my truck at the dealership before we go to the spot. While Sade is driving, she decides to FaceTime Chad because she want to tell him how her wedding dress search went.

"Hey babe!" Chad say as he answered the phone.

"Hey my love, I think I found my dress."

"Really? You think you found your wedding date too?" Chad laughs as he replies to Sade.

"Ha Ha! You ain't funny, baby. Well I was just calling before Maya got in the car. She is dropping her car off at the dealership and then we are going to hangout for a minute. I will see you when I get home." Sade and Chad hang up the phone just before Sade pulls up to get me.

"Bishhhhhh!! I got some tea for you and you bet not say a damn thing," I say to Sade as I get in the truck. "Uhm ok what?" Sade looks at me like something is wrong with me. I go on to tell Sade about the conversation that I had with Dani. I go on to tell her that Dani told me that she is messing with a married man and now she is pregnant. I don't tell Sade at first who the married man is because I want to make sure that Sade has taken in everything about the story before knowing who the guy is.

"Wait! Your sister Dani is messing with a married man?" Sade asks.

"Yes, Bish! That is exactly what I said."

"And she is pregnant?"

"Yes, Bish!"

"I mean your sister don't even like kids so how is she pregnant?" We go back and forth for a while before I finally reveal who this mystery married man is. Although I know Dani will be mad that I told someone about her pregnancy and her relationship, I know that I can trust Sade.

"Ok, so do you know who the guy is? Did she tell you?" Sade asks.

"Jordan, Bish!" I say as I place my hand over my face.

Shocked as hell, Sade stops the damn car and pulls over onto the side of the road. She just cannot believe what she is hearing and really thinks I am being funny.

"Girl, stop lying. Who is the dude forreal?"

I look at Sade and tell her I wish I was just joking but, it is true that Dani has been having an affair with Jordan for years, and now she has gotten pregnant by him.

Sade pulls back on the road and start back driving and shakes her head at me and says, "See, that is the very reason why I can't even trust these bitches around my man." We are going back and forth about how trifling Jordan and Dani are. Sade goes on to tell me that she understands that Dani is my sister, but she has lost all respect for her and she is putting her out of her wedding party.

Everyone but Dani has arrived at the hangout spot. Sade is kind of glad she is not here because she doesn't think she will be able to control her facial expressions or telling her that she can no longer be in her wedding as a Bridesmaid. As Sade and the rest of us are being seated, we are interrupted by Jordan and Chad, who of course is not invited.

"What's up baby?" Chad say as he kisses Sade on the forehead.

"Hey Baby! What are y'all two up to?" Sade say as she gives Jordan the side eye look. Jordan frowns at Sade and is wondering why she is looking at him all crazy.

Jordan has no idea that Dani revealed to me that they have been in a secret relationship for some years. He still thinks nobody knows because he always told Dani that even if they do reach a rough patch, nothing should ever make them reveal that they have been seeing each other. I guess he should've put in the disclosure about getting pregnant as well. Jordan haven't seen Dani in a few weeks, so he is just in the dark about everything when it comes to this pregnancy and their secret relationship.

"Sade, what's up, mane? Why you looking at me like I have done something to you?" Jordan says as he is laughing and shaking his head at Sade.

"Some shit just can't be explained." Sade turns and looks at me as I head back to the table from the bathroom. I had no idea Jordan and Chad had come in. So, when I sit down, I notice that Jordan is standing right in front of me. I can't help but to utter, "This sorry mother fucker."

"What's up Chad?" I asked. You know you should watch who you hang out with because their sorry and cheating ways could rub off on you."

Chad laughs.

"Maya, do you ever shut the hell up? Or you got something hiding in you that you just scared to tell me?" Jordan say as he winks his eye at her.

"Nigga, I barely even want to look at your dumb ass let alone try to tell you something." I ended that real quick.

We both are going back and forth when Dani and Kendall walk in. I knew Dani was coming and was bringing the guy she has been seeing for some time. I am just so eager to see how Jordan is going to react to seeing Dani being with someone else. I thought about warning Dani about Jordan but then I realized that I am still so damn disappointed in her that she probably deserved to get whatever she gets from his stupid ass.

As Dani gets closer, she notices Jordan is talking to Chad and the bartender. She feels butterflies every time she sees him, and she knows that he is the man that her heart belongs to but also knows that even though her heart belongs to him, he belongs to someone else. So, to avoid an encounter with him, Dani decides to just sit at an open table with hopes of not running into Jordan at all. Unfortunately, that plan don't work because just as soon as they are getting ready to sit down at a table on the other side, I yell out, "Hey Dani, we are over here!" Dani look at Kendall and say, "I just want some alone time with you and enjoy you tonight rather than being with all of them."

****

The early morning sunlight beams into the open blinds in Sade and Chad's apartment. Chad always wakes up and give Sade a kiss on her forehead even if she is awake or not. Of course, Sade has been up hours because she can't sleep for thinking about the news that I told her about Dani and Jordan. Sade raise up and ask Chad if he knew that Jordan and Dani have been messing around for years. Chad damn near chokes brushing his teeth because he now wonders how in the hell she knows. Chad knows he can't lie to the woman he has been honest with since the beginning. And he knows that if she knows then she knows that he knows.

"Baby, who told you that?" Chad say as he washes the toothpaste from his mouth.

"Is it true or not?"

"Yes baby!"

"So, you knew, and you never told me?"

"Baby that is not our business, and I never entertained it. When he told me, I told him that was fucked up, but I can't tell a grown man what to do. I didn't tell you because I didn't want you in any drama. I knew that you were best friends with both British and Dani. Then I didn't want you to think that because I knew, it was who I am, too." Chad says as he gets back on the bed next to Sade.

Sade never not once felt like she couldn't trust Chad, however, she does hate that Jordan is his best friend. Sade leans on Chad and tells him that she never wants him to think that she doesn't trust him. But the reason she is not in a hurry to have the wedding is because she is scared that their relationship will be tarnished like all their friend's marriages. Chad assures Sade that he knows she loves him, and he understands where she is coming from but wants her to know that he is his own person and would never put her through the things Jordan put British through.

As they continue to talk, Sade asks Chad will it be wrong to tell Dani that she doesn't want her to stand beside her as a bridesmaid. She also tells Chad that she knows she can't choose his groomsmen but if she had a choice, she would not allow Jordan to be Chad's best man either.

Chad and Sade finish up their conversation so they can get up and get ready to meet the event planner for their upcoming engagement party. Although Sade really hasn't been in a hurry to plan her wedding, she is excited about planning the engagement party. She has been so excited to have both sides of their families get together along with their friends. Both Chad and Sade have been looking forward to their engagement party since they have been engaged.

After Chad and Sade finish meeting with the event planner and getting everything planned out for the engagement party, Chad drops Sade back off at home and he heads to start his day at the shop.

As Sade is walking in, I am pulling up as well. Sade has gotten closer to me since we have been staying in the same building, and we see each other more than anyone else. While in the elevator, I ask Sade if she could use a drink. And of course, Sade is not turning down drinks. She ends up at my house.

We both sit our things down, and head to the wet bar that I have in my apartment. Just as soon as we start to pour drinks, Ricky calls out to me while simultaneously banging on my door. I can't help but laugh at Ricky. I know that every time he does something crazy like that, he has some tea to release. I sit my glass down and go open the door for Ricky.

"Bish, we need to talk!" he says all out of breath. "Oh, hey Shade," he says to Sade throwing his hand up. Ricky calls her Shade because everyone says that she throws the most shade to be so quiet.

"Okay Ricky, so what is it? You are breathing like you have been running for your life," I say as I go to pour him a drink. He sat down with us and went on to say how he was just at the park doing some thinking as he normally does and just as he was about to play on the monkey bars, the birdie told him to look to the left. He says that he saw something that he doesn't believe is Christian-like.

"Bish, I seen Dani and Jordan walking down the hill coming out of the woods. Now I know neither one of them do any hiking so I damn sure know that there could only be one thing they were doing," Ricky say as he takes a sip.

Sade looks at him and says, "So you think they were having sex in the woods?"

"Naw, Shade! I don't think they will do a such thing. I just think they went in the woods to pray," Ricky said so sarcastically. "Bish, what else you think I am saying they were doing?"

Me and Sade look at each other and laugh. I shook my head and told Ricky that Dani told me that her and Jordan have been messing off for 4 years, and she is now pregnant by him.

Ricky just can't believe what he is hearing. He pauses for several minutes, takes several sips, and pauses for one more minute.

"This whole damn group of friends is dysfunctional!"

Ricky lifts the whole damn bottle and turns it up to drink. I tap Ricky on the shoulder and tell him that I agree. He kept drinking, but then stopped to look at me and says, "Wait, so we really have two stories that we can release on Jordan? Girl, we are about to get paid on Jordan broke ass," Ricky laughs saying to me.

Ricky and I have been friends for a very long time, and I know that I can trust him with valuable information. Although I know he is hungry for stories, I know I can trust him not to release any information without my permission. I have really been taking some time to think hard about all the information that I have found out about Jordan. I hate Jordan so bad; I will release a story on him for free. However, not only do I have to think about hurting my best friend, British, I now must think about my own sister, Dani.

Ricky put his drink down and just looked at me. Of course, I know why Ricky is looking at me, but I just did not want to entertain the thought of him wanting to know why I haven't released the stories I have on Jordan. I tell Ricky that it is more to just hurting and making Jordan look bad. I even voiced how I can care less what image he gets. My concern is not for Jordan. It is for my sister and best friend.

Ricky is the type of person who can care less about anyone's feelings. If a story needs to be told, he wants to tell it whether it hurt someone's feelings or not. He goes on to tell me this is why you can't mix business with personal because you will be the one left out in the cold every time.

Sade looks at me and says that Ricky has a point. Although Dani is my sister, she deserves to have some kind of hurt behind what she has done. Not only did she sleep around with her best friend's husband, she gets pregnant by him and she is still messing with him.

Sade stand up in front of me and say, "Girl, I know Dani is your sister but Dani knew what she was doing, and she didn't care if British's feelings were hurt so why should anyone care about her feelings?" I can see how much this is bothering Sade. "Well, I don't care about her feelings and really don't care to be around her anymore either. That is why I am telling her she cannot be in my wedding." Sade says, gathering her things so she can go home.

"But Sade, you act like she slept with your man or something," I say laughing.

"Well real friends put bitches in their place. Second, I am not going to keep her around long enough for her to make Chad her next target," Sade says to me as she walked out the door.

Ricky is still sipping on his drink, but he looks over at me and says, "I mean she is right, Girl. And you still broke so you need to be making a decision because, Bish them 30 days are about over."

"Shut up Ricky." I just can't help but to know that both Sade and Ricky are right, and I do need to hurry up and make a decision about my job. What I am praying about was for something else to hit that does not involve my friend or my sister.

As the night starts to come to an end for me, I sip on my last drop of wine and come to the conclusion that I need to have a talk with Dani to let her know what is going on, especially since we are sisters. I don't want to have Dani blindsided at all. I opened my text message app and reply to Dani's last text.

"Hey sis! I know you think I am mad at you and for the first time you guessed right. I am super-hot at you, but you can't help who you love. Even though sometimes the one your heart loves have you looking stupid.

I really don't know what you see in Jordan, but we are different. I don't know why your heart will allow you to love someone's else husband and you be okay with that. You told me that I don't know Jordan like you do, and I should not judge either of you. I am not judging but, Jordan has a lot of secrets that I know you do not know about. Jordan is a charmer and has always had his way with the ladies. For some reason, the clown knows how to ease his way into someone's heart. You say that you guys are meant to be together, but I just do not know how you think that God will give you another woman's husband. And not just any woman, your best friend's husband. You are my sister, and I love you to death. Nothing you do will ever change that. No matter how I disagree with what you are doing, I will always love you and be here for you. I really hope that you are not pregnant, especially since you have seemed to have met this nice, single guy who adores you. But if you are pregnant, that will be something that I will have to help you get through. But Lord knows I hope you are not. I really do think you should sit down and talk to British about it, and let her know what is going on before the shit hits the fan and you won't have a chance to tell your side of the story. I mean she is going to beat your ass regardless but at least you will have your side told. Anywhoo, I know you are probably sleep right now so let's schedule lunch tomorrow. Love you and talk to you later."

I sent the message and I kind of feel better. I get in the bed, hit my clap on and try to go to sleep. I always sleep well because I know I am single and don't have to wonder if I am with a man who is cheating on me while I am at home.

****

Top of the morning! Sade can't help but get on up after snoozing her alarm 3 times. Chad rolls over and say to his beautiful fiancé, "Baby how many times are you going to hit that button?" Sade looked at Chad. "However long it takes me to get the nerve to get up and have this conversation with the Hoe-ni," she said.

"Who?" Chad raises up and asks.

"I'm sorry! I am talking about Dani. I have decided that I was going to just tell her that she will no longer be in our wedding, and she is no longer invited to our engagement party."

Chad leans over to Sade and says, "Baby, I know that you are mad, but she is still your friend. I get you do not want her in the wedding but let her still be able to come to the party. I mean, at least get her gift anyway."
They just look at each other and laugh. The one thing that Sade loves about Chad is that he is someone that she can laugh with and be herself around. She and Chad are inseparable and she knows that despite everything her friends have going on in their marriages, she has a good man, and she is not going to let what she sees get in the way of marrying her best friend.

Sade finally get the nerve to send Dani a text and ask her if she can meet her for lunch. Just as Sade puts her phone down, there was an alert. Dani did not hesitate to text back and say ok. She told Sade that I wanted to meet as well. So the three of us can just all meet at the same time. Sade is not opposed to having the meeting with me as well since I am the one who told her about the relationship between Jordan and Dani and the fact that she had already told me how she feel about Dani being in her wedding.

Sade replies to Dani, "Cool beans."

They arrived at our meeting spot, and of course Sade and Dani arrived at the same time. It is not hard for Dani to realize that something is wrong with Sade.

"Hey Girl!" Dani says to Sade. "You want to go ahead and sit while we wait on Maya to get here?"

"Yea, we can. You know Maya is always late anyway and besides I won't be here long anyway," Sade replies to Dani.

"Is everything ok? Girl, you talk like you don't want to be with me like I did something to you."

"No! You didn't do anything to me, but I do want to talk to you about something that I have only spoke to Maya about." Sade get her purse while she gets up and head to an empty table on the patio.

Sade and Dani order them a drink, and Sade whispers to the waitress that she needs to have it very strong. Dani hears what Sade says and she becomes nervous about what Sade really wants to talk to her about.

Sade look at Dani and tells her that she is just going to get straight to the point.

"So, you know my wedding is coming up, and I am super excited about it. What I am excited the most about is that my friends will be by my side as I say 'I Do' to the man that I know God created just for me."

Dani smiles at Sade and replies, "You know I am so happy for you, and I will be right beside you."

Sade can't help but to turn her glass up to make sure she gets every drop of alcohol out that glass.

"Dani, I would say that I am sorry, but I am truly not. I just cannot have you in my wedding. You are not the friend that I thought you were, and I refused to have someone stand beside me who is not truthful to themselves."

Dani stops Sade in mid-sentence and ask her what she is talking about, and how does she feel she is not capable of being in her wedding. Just as Sade is about to answer her question, I walk up to the table and sit down. When Dani saw the look on my face, she knew then that I had shared what she told me in confidence with Sade.

"Look Dani, we are still cool, but I can't have your trifling ass in my wedding. I can't have someone stand beside me who is sleeping with a married man. How do I know you will not try to sleep with my man? Sorry boo, I just can't deal with someone like you. If you still want to come to the engagement party, you are more than welcome. But consider yourself out of my wedding."

Dani had the most hurtful look on her face because she always considered Sade to be the one friend she was closest to and more real than any of us.

Nikki

Top of the morning and Nikki is over her career as a Lawyer. As she sits back in her chair going over her current cases, her assistant walks in to let her know that she has a phone call on line 2.

"Hello, this is Nicole," she answers all professionally.

"Yes ma'am, I am looking for someone to accompany me to my company's Gala, and I'm just wondering if you could be my date?" The caller asks. Nikki is smiling, and she can't help but to laugh at the things her new victim will always call and say.

Nikki is one of the top attorneys in the city and is working for the largest law office in the state. She is the one out of all of us who doesn't want to be in a committed relationship and would only want to date a man who was either in a relationship, married, or just wants to be friends with benefits. This is her choice because if a man is in either category, then she can still do what she wants to do and doesn't have to be tied down to one man. She has several victims, and depending on her mood for the day, it will determine who she will be with on that day. At this present time, she has her eye on someone in her firm. But she has recently met someone else.

As Nikki gets ready to go, she actually cannot wait to get home to have a little fun with the guy she has been seeing for the past few months. She gets home to find a note on her door that read, "Be naked when I get back." "Ahhh shit! This boy about to get it," Nikki says as she hurries to turn her key and enter into her house.

Shortly after she showers and puts on her robe, she hear that sexy knock at her door. Without even looking out the peep hole, she opens it right on up because only one person has that knock.

"What's up sexy?" Nikki says as she takes the guy by his jacket and pulls him right on in.

They start to kiss, and Nikki's red silk robe eventually slides down her yellow, soft skin, toned body onto the floor. What Nikki likes most about this man is that he is sexy, yellow like the sun, good in bed, and will have sex anywhere.

After having hot and sweaty sex, Nikki got up and said, "Now ain't you glad you chose me?"

He said, "You chose me!"

So, let's rewind back to Girl's Trip in Hawaii. Nikki had already made up in her mind that she was going to Hawaii to do more than just have fun on the trip -- from the time she got off the plane until the time she spotted her first victim at the bar. Little did she know, just a few hours later this fine dude would capture her attention.

While Nikki and the rest of us girls were on the beach, there was a group of guys who were also there, and one of those guys made Nikki forget all about Victim #1. She constantly kept looking at the guy all flirty-like, so he would know that she was interested in him. When she saw him walking in her direction, she immediately started getting herself together.

"Hello Ladies," the fine guy said to all them. Everyone spoke except for British. She just sat there blushing.

"Can I borrow your girl for a moment?" He asked as he reached for British's hand.

Nikki could not believe she had been rejected. So she sat back down all cool and continued to drink on her

Sex on the Beach. Although he left with British, Nikki was still attracted to him and seemed to not even care that he was interested in her best friend.

On that same night, Nikki went to the steam room on the beach. As she was enjoying the steam, in walked the fine guy she was attracted to. Nikki didn't know if she was seeing things because she had several drinks or if this guy was really there. He and Nikki sat across from each other and constantly looked at one another flirtatious.

"I'm Phil and you are?" he said as he got up to shake Nikki's hand.

"I'm Nikki, British's best friend," Nikki said as she gave him a small smirk.

Minutes later, robes were on the floor and Nikki and Phil were having sex as steam arose from their sweaty bodies. When they were done, Phil whispered in Nikki's ear and told her she just may be as good as her friend. They exchanged numbers, something he didn't even do with British, and said that they would keep in touch when they left Hawaii. When they walked out, they both went in two different directions like nothing even happened.

When it was time to depart Hawaii, British could not understand why she had not heard from Phil since their sexual encounter on the beach the night before. Although Nikki knew what she had done and knew why Phil did not reach out, she kept it cool and played as if British should just enjoy the brief moment they had and not to even worry about it. British knew Nikki was right, however, with sex like that, British knew it would be hard to forget.

However, as promised, Nikki and Phil stayed in touch. They actually were together the same night they returned home. Nikki was Nikki and the way she saw it, he was not British's man to begin with.

The night had come to attend Phil's company's Gala. What was going to be different for Nikki is that she does not go out in public with the men she sleeps with. Why? Because they are usually married or in a relationship.

Phil was very different from the guys Nikki normally talked to. He was actually single, but he and Nikki just enjoyed being with each other and really didn't want anything serious.

Nikki got dressed and headed out the door. Phil had arranged for the company car to pick her up. He was a CFO at one of the largest companies in the United States.

As Nikki arrived at the venue, Phil waited outside to escort her in. They locked arms and began walking up the stairs to enter the inside. Nikki had on a long red sequin gown that matched Phil's black tux with red lining. When they got inside, they were greeted by some of Phil's colleagues. Of course because Nikki worked for a well-known law firm, several people at the Gala knew who she was. To everyone else, Nikki and Phil made a cute couple but to them they were the best of fuck buddies who just wanted to have fun and enjoy life for what it is.

After the gala, they left and headed to Phil's home. On the way there, Nikki received a phone call from British.

"Hey girl! What's up?" Nikki answered while looking at Phil.

"Bish, so I was looking on Facebook and I guess who I see?" British asked.

"Who?"

"Phil!"

"Oh!" Nikki bucked her eyes. "Where was he?"

"So, come to find out he is a CFO at the company he works for, and the reason why I couldn't find him on Facebook by Phil is because Phil is a nickname," British said sarcastically.

Nikki turned her head and asked, "What do you mean?"

"Well this post has another name tagged but with his picture. Turns out his name is Philander."

"Oh ok!" Girl let me call you back," Nikki rushed off the phone.

Nikki knew Phil did not hear their conversation because he was too busy on his phone and was not paying attention. To be honest, she really didn't care what his real name was as long as the sex was good, and he kept it coming every time she wanted it.

113

Nikki didn't even bother to share the conversation with him once they arrived at his house. This was the first time Nikki had been to Phil's house because he was always popping up at her house. As they stepped out the car and went in, Nikki thought to herself, "Damn! This nigga living it up."

Nikki put her coat and purse down and as she is getting ready to sit down on the couch, she was interrupted by Phil saying to her, "Nahh, get yo' ass up them stairs. I'm about to snatch that damn dress off you."

The reason Nikki is feeling Phil so much is because she loves how he talks to her when they are getting ready to have sex. Nikki is a freak at heart, and Phil is definitely the match she needs. Phil does not take it easy on Nikki. He grabs her by her hair, he slaps her on her ass, and most of all, he loves tossing her nicely firm ass in the air.

As the moans start, Nikki gets on top and rides Phil just like he likes. Per usual, he grabs Nikki by her ass and bounces her up and down. Nikki knows how to ride to keep Phil's mouth wide open while he moans. Phil then grabs Nikki and flips her over where he is behind her, pulling her up on her knees and archs her back. While he is stroking, he fingers her. Nikki can't ever fight the urge to not scream. First nut, "Ohhh shit baby!" Nikki says as her knees begin to get weak, but she keeps going because she is a solider. Nikki then falls on her stomach and began giving it to Phil, his favorite position. She knows how to move in the right direction at the right rate of speed.

"Ahhhhh fuuuuckkkk!" Phil screams. There that shit go, Nikki says to herself. Phil falls out.

"Damn Boo! Did you miss me, or you got something you want to tell me?" Phil wipes his sweat and says to Nikki.

Nikki loves how Phil enjoys the sex she gives to him. Neither one of them are boring in the bedroom. She knows that he just can't get enough of her. He rests up for about 15 minutes was ready to go for another round. Of course Nikki does not mind because she is ready too.

As they are finishing up their third round, Nikki tells Phil that she has to get ready to go home because she has an early morning that she has to get ready for. He wants her to spend the night, but in true Nikki fashion, she does not want to wake up in someone else's bed. That is her motto to herself.

"So how long do you think you can keep this little secret from your best friend?" Phil asks as he gets his naked ass out of the bed and heads to the bathroom to start his shower.

With no concern in the world, Nikki tells Phil that she is not trying to keep it a secret, it is just none of anyone's business, and if they were exclusive then she would come right out and tell her. She knows that she can say those things to him because she knows that he does not want to be in a relationship. So he will agree with whatever she decides. However, Nikki has been thinking about these pictures she and Phil were taking at the Gala last night. Nikki just says to herself that she will just deal with that when it comes.

The sun is coming up, and Nikki gets ready to meet Toya and British. She promised Toya that she would go with her to look at some homes that are for sale.

Although Toya is saying that both she and her husband are looking to purchase another home, Nikki can't help but to think that something is going on in Toya's marriage that she is not telling us.

Toya always speaks highly of her marriage like they don't ever have any problems, but we all know that ain't nobody marriage or relationship *that* perfect. It is believed that is the reason why she is always trying to find fault in everyone else's relationship -- to keep us from noticing what is really going on in hers.

British takes us to the homes that she pulled up, and of course Toya's old ass don't like either one of them. Nikki tells British that she doesn't even see why she bothered to pull up any because Toya's grandma taste is very much old-fashioned.

Nikki puts the address into the GPS of one home that she had found on the realtor site. We drive and finally pull up to this white bricked house that looks as if it had no upgrades. When we got ready to go look inside the house, British noticed that the home was a foreclosure home.

"Toya, you do know this is a foreclosure home right?" British asks Toya as she is showing her the iPad.

"Yes, and you do know that it is only $150,000 right?" Toya replied back to British frowning.

British can't help but give Nikki this funny look, and they both are wondering why Toya would sell her big, nice home for a home that is much smaller and doesn't look worth purchasing. They all proceed to walk into the home. Entering, they see the walls all painted different colors, the carpet is filthy, there are no upgrades, and the light fixtures are horrible.

"Okay, Bish! Your husband must be putting your ass out?" Nikki burst out and asks Toya.

She looks at Nikki wanting to just slap her. "No sweetheart, we just want to sell our home and move into something new."

"So this is what you call something new? Bish stop lying and tell us the truth."

"Why would my husband be putting me out though? I am the bread winner." Toya rolls her eyes at Nikki and keeps looking throughout the home.

British and Nikki just stand to the side and let Toya look at whatever she needed to look at. Toya finally finishes looking at the raggedy ass home, and they head on to the next home on the list.

While riding, Nikki turns around and looks at Toya and say, "Okay girl, you ready to tell us why you wasting our time looking at raggedy houses and shit?"

"If I tell you, will you promise to shut the hell up?" Toya said.

Nikki turns all the way around and responds, "Yeeees Girl, Yes!"

"I'm purchasing a hoe house for hoes like you to come to and not be judged. Now turn around and shut the hell up." Toya can't help but to be sarcastic with Nikki.

"Well hell, you need me to do the picking out because your country ass can't even pick out a house hoes will enjoy." Nikki sips on her drink and turns around.

Nikki gets a phone call and she immediately answers and tells the person on the other end that she will call them back once she gets home. She hates to miss the call because she knows it is Phil wanting some mid-day ass, and she don't have the time to be explaining to Nikki and Toya why she is doing what she is doing and *who* she is doing.

"So Brit, how are things going with you and Jayden?" Nikki tries to hurry up and spark a conversation so neither Toya nor British will ask her who was calling.

"Girl, we can't be better. I mean he is everything I want, didn't have and need. I mean it's like falling in love with most the unexpected person. I thank God for that night. Just thinking that I almost didn't go out with y'all because Jordan had made me so damn mad. I would've missed out on love," British smiles and says.

"Okay bish, so you in *love* love? Like poetry in love? Like you about to be sprung in love?" Nikki laughs and says.

Although we all joke and laugh at how British has been on cloud nine with Jayden, we are all glad she is getting over Jordan's cheating and lying ass. We don't really see British as much as we used to because she and Jayden spend a lot of time together. I am proud of my girl. After British finished telling Nikki and Toya how happy Jayden makes her, she asks Nikki who is she currently entertaining. Nikki damn near chokes on the orange Fanta she was drinking.

"How you figure I am entertaining someone?"

"Trick, there is never a time when you not getting no dick," British laughs and replies.

"Well I got this lil junt that has been keeping my juices and berries going," Nikki says.

"Oh okay then! So, who is this fella?"

"I got to keep this fella a little secret for now because he so damn fine, I don't want none of y'all thirsty asses forgetting y'all got niggas. And I may just have to keep this one."

"Keep him?" British replies all sarcastically.

"Girl yes. He is single and he does things that I ain't even used to."

"Single? Bitch you not even attracted to single men."

"That's why this one just may be the one to change my life. He is single, fine, and the sex have me reaching for shit that ain't even there."

"Damn!"

"Right. So yes, I am keeping this one all to myself for a while," Nikki says as she picks up her phone to text Phil nasty little text messages to get him in the mood.

By now, Nikki and British are tired of looking at houses with Toya, so of course, it is time for drinks. Toya sends out a text message to all of us to see if everyone is down with meeting at the bar. I am so over this day, so I hurry up and reply back yes and let Toya know that I will be in route. I pull up to the valet parking right behind British's Range Rover. We all walk in together and who do we see as soon as we enter the door? Jordan's trifling ass! British walked right on by his ass like she didn't even see him sitting there. Jordan tries his best to play hard so we won't know that he is dying on the inside without British, but we all know the bastard can't survive without her.

Toya's nice ass gets close enough so she can speak and give him a hug. Nikki's crazy ass walks by him and say, "Damn Bruh, you wife walked passed yo' ass like you Casper." Nikki just laughed in his face and keep on walking. Me? I can't stand the helpless bastard. I give him the, "Don't say shit to me," look and keep walking past his ass like British did. Did I already mention that I can't stand his ass? We have never gotten along. If it was up to me, British would not have wasted her time on such a loser.

Nikki's petty ass hurries up and sits her purse down so she could start the talk about Jordan.

"Damn, Bish! Did you even see Jordan?" Nikki asks British laughing.

"Jordan? All I see is one man and that man is walking this way right now." British gets up from the table and hugs Jayden. They were just so cute together. Jayden came around and gave each one of us a hug. We absolutely love Jayden for British. Hell, to be honest, I think I will love anybody other than Jordan. Jayden sits next to British. Of course, here comes Jordan ass walking with Chad. Chad speaks to everyone and sits next to Sade.

"Jordan where are you going to sit?" Sade asks

"I was planning on sitting beside my wife but there is someone sitting in the wrong chair," Jordan replies looking at British and Jayden.

Nikki damn near chokes on her drink and says, "Bruh, who sitting in the wrong chair?" I was ready to hear his response. Jordan has always been the man that talks a whole lot of shit like he so bad, and his ugly ass ain't gon' buss a grape. So I look at Jordan and ask in such a sweet voice, "Yes Jordan, who is in your seat and who is your wife?" I didn't even bother to look at British to see what's her reaction to his foolery because I already know that she is unbothered.

"Oh, my bad my guy! You can have this seat," Jayden says as he gets up to give Jordan the seat.

Jordan walks over and mumbles, "Yea that's what I'm talking about."

Jayden walks over to the other side of British and takes her by her hand and says, "Y,all enjoy the rest of your night. Me and my woman going home."

British can't do nothing but give Jordan this hilarious smirk and walk away. Everyone at the table just burst out laughing.

Nikki looks at Jordan and says, "Mane they just shitted on you."

Typical Jordan, he gon' always make it seem like he ain't hurting. Hell, that shit hurt my feelings, and it wasn't even directed towards me. I really do get a kick out of laughing at Jordan during this time because he has done British so wrong over the years. Now he look like a complete fool because she ain't stuttin' his ass.

As we all continue to talk, Jordan's ass is just drinking -- so damn funny to me. His phone rings and he answers and tells the person on the other end that he was on his way. I am 100% sure that it is some hoe that he met online somewhere. So he get up and leaves. As soon as he is walking out the door, here comes my sister and Kendall walking in. Boom! Another humiliation in his face. The thing about Jordan and Dani is that I really do believe that Dani is crazy in love with Jordan and will leave Kendall for Jordan's ass.

Nikki gets a text on her phone and tells me that she is about to head home. Looks like she got a booty call too. Hell, everybody got a booty call but my ass. Oh well, let me get my lonely ass home and enjoy some alone time.

Nikki arrives homes and there Phil sits on the bench that she has outside of her door. As Nikki is trying to unlock and open her door, Phil slams her up against the wall and pulls up her dress. This is why Nikki craves Phil so much. He is always spontaneous like that. Even though Nikki lives in an apartment and there are people in and out, Nikki is always up to doing anything Phil wants to do when it comes to sex.

Phil pulls Nikki by her hair and sticks it in and start fucking her. She tries her best not to moan loud so her neighbors won't hear her. As she struggles to unlock the door, Phil lets up to give her a break.

"What took you so long?" Phil asks as he continue to kiss Nikki on her neck.

"I know when I make you wait, you give it to me even better," Nikki say as she takes Phil clothes off.

Without any hesitation, they both just fall to the floor and continue having sex until they are interrupted by a knock at the door by yours truly.

"Fuck! Who you got coming over here?" Phil said as he continued to hit it from the back.

"I don't know and I don't care. They will get the point and leave," Nikki struggles to say in between her moaning.

"Bitch, I know you hear me knocking," I say as I start to bang on the door.

My nosey ass put my ear to the door to see if I can hear any movement. "Trick, are you fucking? I hear yo' fat ass struggling to breath." I keep banging on the door. Phil finally stopped and asks Nikki who the hell is that at the door. Nikki rolls her eyes and tells Phil to go to the back until she gets rid of me. Rid of me? Well that's what she thinks anyway.

"Maya, what do you want? I am busy. I just left your ass."

"I know but hell I ain't got no man to go home and fuck. So since you ain't really got a man, it's not fair for you to come home and get some either," I say to her and move her little ass out the way and walked on in.

I look around and don't see anyone, but I know she is doing the same thing that was done outside of her front door because that same funky sex smell is also in her living room.

"So, who is your victim today? Where he at Nikki?"

"Maya, yes I am currently getting fucked, and I want to go back to it. I am so sorry that don't nobody wanna give you none. But I need you to leave so I can go back to fucking please."

"Girl, I ain't about to go nowhere, hell," I say as I attempt to sit down on her couch.

"Bitch, get your ass up out of here. I love you but, you got to go." Nikki grabs me by my arm and put me out of the door. This trick is strong, because right now I am looking at the peep hole on her door which means she just put my ass up out of there for real. I don't know whether I should be mad or not, but whomever is up in that house must be really good because that bish didn't even care about our friendship in that moment! LOL! I guess I better take my lonely ass home then and eat some ice cream or something until one of these bishes is finished.

"Who was at the door?" Phil ask Nikki as she climbs back on top of him.

"That was Maya nosey ass. She is always trying to figure out who I am fucking," Nikki says as she tries to hush Phil up from asking questions so they could get back to it.

As the bright sunshine peek into Nikki's blinds, she realizes that for the first time, she did not kick out the nigga she slept with the night before. It is just something about Phil. He brings a lot to Nikki's table. She gets up and goes into the kitchen and starts making breakfast. Oh, this bish must be in love for real because she don't even make breakfast for herself.

As Nikki is standing over the stove whipping the eggs, she feels Phil come up behind her rubbing on her ass and kissing her on the neck.

"Smells good baby," Phil says as he bends her over the stove, pulls up the dress she slept in and sticks his man in.

When they finish with their quickie, she fixes their plates. After breakfast, they shower together. I mean no matter where they are, they are going to have sex. Sex in the shower, then sex trying to put on their clothes! So back in the shower they go! Finally their clothes are on and they both head out to start their day.

Nikki walks into her office where she is met with her little 25 year-old boy toy that she has been messing with sitting on her couch in her office. As she walks over and sits her briefcase on her desk, she looks at Justin and asks him what does he want. Justin gets up and ask Nikki why hasn't he heard from her in weeks. Nikki responds by telling him that she didn't know he was her daddy.

"That's not what you say when you are bent over screaming "Daaadddy," Justin says as he pulls her neck back by her hair.

"Well looks like you still have milk or something in your ears because I don't be screaming DAAAADDDYYY, I be screaming ZAAAADYY. There's a difference," Nikki says as she closes her door. "Now get over here and fuck me."

Justin is an intern at the office and when he walked in on his first day, Nikki knew she was going to make him her play toy. Nikki would always call Justin in her office just for a quickie from time to time. Since he is only 25, he ain't graduated to coming to her house or any other place outside of the office. He is good at satisfying her, but he does not please her like Phil does.

Justin lifts Nikki up and lays her across her desk and starts giving her head. What Nikki loves about Justin is that he takes his time when he is giving head and gives her the orgasm she needs at the very moment. She likes that he puts his all in trying to please her so she can pretty much do anything to him. Justin has a girlfriend at home, who comes into the office often to bring him lunch. While Justin has Nikki bent over her desk fucking her from the back, he looks out the blinds to see his girlfriend walking down the hall looking for him. "Fuck!" Justin say as he quickly pulls up his pants and runs to the blinds in Nikki's office. "My girl brought her ass up here again!"

"Oh! Let's see what Betty Boop bought us for lunch today," Nikki says laughing, pulling her dress down and running to the door.

"Sit yo petty ass down!" Justin says and walks out of her office.

Nikki stands in her doorway and watches Justin hug and kiss his girlfriend. Nikki laughs in her head because it is so funny to her how these women really be thinking they have a good man. This is the very reason why she does not want to be committed to a man because she knows how men are. She knows that a man is one way at home but a totally different person when they are in the streets. Here Justin is, hugging and kissing his girlfriend, she is blushing because Justin is parading her around the office like he is the happiest man alive, and he just finished fucking in the office. Nikki just laughed and heads to the bathroom to freshen up. She has to walk right by Justin and his girlfriend.

"OMG, I just love your shoes! Oh baby, you have to buy me some of those," Justin's girlfriend says as they are walking by each other.

Justin gives this smirk and looks at Nikki as she replies, "Oh, yes Justin you have to get your girlfriend some of these. I know you just love these shoes."

Nikki laughs and continues to walk. It is so funny because Justin purchased those shoes for Nikki for her birthday. His clueless girlfriend has absolutely no idea how much she and Justin fuck in the office on a regular, I mean like fucking every day the office is open and sometimes when the office is closed. If she is going in to work on some files, she calls Justin to meet her there.

While Nikki is in the bathroom freshening up, Justin's girlfriend walks in. She walks up to the sink where Nikki is fixing her hair. "Hey, I didn't get your name. Justin introduced me to everyone but you," she says as she is washing her hands looking in the mirror at Nikki.

"My name is Nikki, and you are?" Nikki replies.

"I'm Jessica, Justin's fiancé."

"Fiancé?" Nikki says laughing. "Justin never said anything about him being engaged. Congratulations! I am going to have to make sure I congratulate him when I get back on the floor."

Nikki dries her hands and starts to walk out of the door, but Jessica interrupts her leaving.

"By any chance, do you know my fiancé in any kind of way? I am asking because it is quite strange that he has introduced me to everyone in the office, but he didn't attempt to introduce me to you. And I noticed that you made that smart comment about him liking your shoes. I am just wondering."

"I met your fiancé on his first day in the office. Is it something you are trying to figure out? Now why your fiancé did not introduce you to me is something you will have to ask him about," Nikki says as she smiles at Jessica and walks out of the door heading back to her office.

Justin is standing outside the door looking like he had seen a ghost. He is wondering if Jessica is trying to figure out if he has something sexual going on with Nikki. She walks by Justin and says "Your fiancé is very nice."

Toya

"I'm so sick of yo' nothing having ass!" Toya says to Austin. "All yo' ass do is sit around the house, drink and do absolutely nothing else."

Toya and her husband Austin have been together for over 20 years and married for more than 10. She really does come off as if she has the perfect marriage and like they don't have any issues in their marriage. They met right after Toya graduated college. She had applied for a position at a bank where Austin was the branch manager. They hit it off quickly. One of the problems Toya and Austin are having is that Toya feels that since Austin is a branch manager, he should be pulling more weight around the house. Toya and Austin never had kids together because Austin had already had 3 kids, that he has custody of, and Toya never really wanted to have children. Another major problem is that Austin wants to have another child, and Toya thinks it best to not add a fourth child to the equation.

"Toya, I'm meeting the guys after work for some drinks. Can you make sure you pick up Malik from basketball practice this evening?" Austin asks as he is getting his keys and leaving out of the door.

She looks at Austin in pure anger and yells, "Hell naw! That's your responsibility. I have something to do."

"What you got to do that you can't pick him up? It ain't that important." Austin says to Toya as he attempts to pull out of the garage.

Toya leans into Austin's car and says, "I said I have something to do, and that is your responsibility. So if you don't pick him up, he will be finding a ride home. You going to the bar drinking is not important. You can pick up your own son from basketball practice."

As Toya is getting ready for work, her phone rings. It's Nikki calling.

"Hello," Toya answers.

"Good Morning, bish! What you up to and why does it sound like something is wrong with you?" Nikki asks.

Toya connects her Bluetooth headset so she can finish getting ready while she tells Nikki what is going on.

"Girl, Austin gon' come downstairs this morning before he leaves for work and tells me that he is going to meet some guys after work for drinks and for me to pick up Malik from basketball practice. I told him hell naw because I have something to do. Don't you know that bastard had the nerve to tell me that what I have to do is not more important than me picking up *his* son from practice? I told him that Malik is *his* responsibility and not mine, and him going to the bar is not important."

"Girl, I know y'all married and all, but who in the hell said step mommies take over all responsibilities? Hell, call his mama and tell her to pick him up. Matter of fact, who is the damn chile mammy anyway?" Nikki asks.

"Girl, she is someone that Austin says left them right after the youngest one was born. He doesn't talk about her and neither do the kids. So I don't ask any questions. I don't want to have to deal with baby mama drama anyway," Toya replies.

Toya goes on to tell Nikki how she is sick of Austin and how sometimes she regrets marrying him. He loves that funky car club he joined years ago, and she believes that he has messed with several women in the car club but just can't prove it. The reason why Toya believes that is because the club has more single women members than men. Toya starts to let it all out without Nikki even asking her.

"I am just so ready to leave his nothing having ass. If it wasn't for him paying these bills and me really loving his children, I would have been gone. I am really thinking about just walking out one day, taking the kids with me and never looking back. He wouldn't care either way. He is just more concerned about that car club and the niggas that he is always hanging with. Hell, sometimes I think he is gay and sleeping with them! Every time you look around, he calling talking about he is at the bar with a nigga. UUUGGHH! Black bastard gets on my darn nerves!"

"Ok bish! I mean I didn't call you for all of that but damn, I think you need a damn blunt. So let me ask you, what is the real reason why you had us looking at homes the other day?" Nikki asks knowing damn well Toya will probably lie again.

"Look, don't say anything to the girls, but yes I am planning on leaving Austin. I am planning on taking the kids with me because I have been in their lives since they were babies and to them, I am their mother. I am just waiting until I find the right home for us and stack some more money up."

"So why the hell you taking his kids though? You don't have any kids. Why do you want to have mother responsibilities? Let that mother fucker take care of his own damn kids."

"Girl! I will not do that. Those kids need me, and just because I didn't birth them does not mean I don't love them like my own."

"Ok Mother Theresa. If that makes you happy."

"Well girl let me finish getting ready for work so I can get out of here, and I will see you this evening at the spot," Toya tells Nikki as they say their goodbyes.

As she continues to get dressed, Toya can't help but think Austin is cheating because he is never really home. They don't have sex like they used to, and when they do have sex, he is really not into it. She knows she wants to leave, but the big issue is what will she do without his kids and what will his kids do without her? As she starts to look for her shoes, she instantly comes out of those thoughts she was having, and she noticed something that was about to change her whole damn day.

"A fucking condom wrapper?" Toya says out loud. "We haven't used condoms in years, so who in the fuck has this bastard had in my bed?" She takes a picture of it, picks it up and leaves it on the nightstand on his side of the bed.

As Toya is driving to work, she gets a call from Austin. She immediately starts asking herself if she wants to go ahead and ask him about the condom or does she just say nothing and let him go home and find it on his nightstand?

"Hello?" Toya answers nonchalantly.

"Baby, don't forget about today, and I am working late so you can just pick you and the kids up something to eat on the way home instead of cooking," Austin responds.

"Sure baby. Have a good day." Toya hangs up the phone.

As Toya was heading into work, she decided to call in for the day. Then she headed to my office. Of course, everyone knows that if it is something that needs to be known, I can find out that information in about 2-4 hours. Yea, I'm that bish that finds out the tea and will bust your ass out on it.

Toya calls me and tells me about what she had found at the house and the phone call that she had received from Austin. She also expresses that she just has that gut feeling that he is cheating but just doesn't know with who. But she knows that I can find out.

"Bish, you know my favorite saying is, if your gut is telling you something, then that's what it is," I said and told her to meet me at the office.

As I walk into the office, my assistant tells me that one of my best friends was waiting in there for me. It was Toya. She was already there!

"Damn girl, was you in the parking lot when you called me, or did you just damn near drive 100 mph to get here?"

Toya is the oldest of us girls, so she always be wanting to do things the Christian way and try to give everyone the benefit of the doubt. I have always thought something weird was going on with her marriage, but let her tell it, she's got the perfect marriage.

Austin just always looks like he got something up his sleeve. That is one sneaky bastard -- his high yellow ass -- can dress his ass off, but something just ain't right about him.

Toya looks at me with them worried eyes, "Girl, what if Austin is not cheating on me and I'm doing all of this for nothing."

"Well if he not cheating, then you just used a vacation day at work for nothing, and I'm gon' beat your ass for having me rushing to work," I said as I sit down and turn on my computer. I couldn't help but to notice that Ricky's ugly ass keeps walking past my office looking in the window. "What the fuck?" I thought to myself and frowned as he walked past once again in the opposite direction from his office.

"Ricky?" I yell trying to get Ricky's attention before he gets too far down the hallway.

"Yes ma'am?" He responds as he pokes his head in my door.

"Umm... are you okay?"

"What do you mean, am I okay?"

"Come in and close my door. I need you to help me find out something."

"How you doing, Ricky?" Toya asks, but he barely acknowledges her.

"Oh hey, Toya. How are you?" Ricky nervously asks.

I'm sitting here looking at Ricky and just can't understand what is up with him today.

"So, why are you here so early, and what are y'all doing?" Ricky asked.

"Well Austin been on some slick shit lately, and Toya is trying to find out if he is cheating or not," I replied as I log into my fake Facebook account.

"Toya, what is he doing for you to think that he is cheating?" Ricky bites his nails as he impatiently waits on Toya to reply.

"I don't know. I just been having these gut feelings lately, and you know what they say, a woman's intuition is always right."

"Aw hell girl, that's just that nasty ass detox tea y'all fat asses been drinking. That man ain't doing nothing." Ricky picks up the folder on my desk that I had for him and walk out the door. I still can't understand why he is acting so damn weird this morning.

As I continue my FaceBook investigation, Toya gets a call from Austin.

"This is Austin. Should I answer?" Toya looks at me asking.

I look at her sideways and respond, "Uh, do you want to talk to the mane or not chile?"

"Hello?" Toya answers

"So why you not at work?" Austin asks Toya sounding all worried and shit.

Toya looks up at me and put her phone on speaker.

"How you know I am not at work?"

"Why the hell you not at work?"

"Because I am grown and if I want to take a day off I can. What's the problem and what the hell you want?"

Both Toya and I kept looking at each other all while trying to figure out how the hell he knew Toya was not at work.

"Where you at?" Austin continues to ask Toya multiple questions.

"I am with Maya." And I am looking at her like, "Don't tell that crazy mofo you with me, because I don't *want* him calling my phone."

Toya hangs up the phone and looks at me with a confused eye. I shake my head and say, "Girl, that fool probably got a tracker on your car."

As Toya leaves my office, I just can't help but to feel sorry for her ass. She is the one who always tries to give everyone else advice on their relationships but can't figure out what to do with hers. Not to mention, she has always been the one to come off as she has the perfect marriage, but I told y'all in the beginning, that bastard ain't shit either.

Night falls and Toya is just still puzzled about what the hell is going on. Dinner cooked; kids are all settled but Austin is still not home. Toya takes her shower and gets her clothes together for the next morning. As she is headed to bed, she hears the door opening downstairs so she peaks her head out of the bedroom door. As she was just about to ask if it was Austin, she hears him on the phone saying he had made it in the house and he would call them tomorrow.

Toya has never been the one to just haul off and ask questions. She has always been the one to gather her information first and then present the facts all at one time. Rather than trying to go downstairs and pop off on Austin's ass, she just went to bed. When he finally comes to the bed, as Toya was trying to close her eyes and go to sleep, she couldn't help but to wonder if her thoughts of Austin cheating were correct.

Toya rolls over and tries to lay on Austin's chest and rub her hands down his leg, but before she could get to "Mr. Willie," he stops her and tell her that he is tired. Of course, she knows that is some bullshit, because every time Austin has some Tequila, he is horny as hell. But she kept it cute and just rolled over and went to sleep.

Austin knows that Toya is onto something, so he just tried to play everything cool and to watch what he says and does. You see, everyone knows that Austin is slow as hell which makes him a dumb ass cheater. How the hell he gon' turn down some ass while he is drunk and she *not* think that he is cheating and getting ass from somewhere else? Damn Dummy.

****

As the sun starts to shine through the windows onto Toya's face, she realizes that she can't sleep in even though it is Saturday. She gets up and heads to the bathroom to take a shower. It does not even phase her that Austin was not in the bed. What she doesn't know is that Austin is downstairs fixing breakfast for her. Pause! So last night he turns down sex and now he is fixing breakfast? This fool! Okay, back to Toya.

As Toya is in the shower, she hears Austin moving things around in the bedroom. Without even acknowledging anything he is doing, she continues with her shower. Austin walks in the bathroom and joins her. She is shocked because he has been ignoring her for weeks. He takes the towel from her and turns her around and places her arms up on the shower wall. He starts to kiss her from the back of her neck down to her butt cheeks. He then starts to rub his fingers across her clitoris just the way she likes. Toya is really enjoying the attention that she is getting from him. He turns her around, suck her titties and then starts to eat her out. He finishes but did not once initiate sex. Toya thought it was kind of odd that he would do all of that but didn't want to have sex.

Toya and Austin get a towel and continue bathing. Austin turns around, and as Toya was attempting to wash his back, she noticed something was in Austin's ass. She paused for a second and looked a little puzzled. She took her hand and pulled out a condom from his ass.

"What the fuck is this?" She yelled out loud. Austin turned around and saw that Toya was holding a used condom in her hand.

"It's not what you think," he said as he took the condom out of Toya's hand.

"This is a condom but why was it stuck in your ass?"

"I can explain," he said.

Toya couldn't say anything else. She just got her towel and stepped out of the shower. Austin was trying his best to go after her, but when he saw her walking towards her nightstand, rather than him continuing to follow her, he just ran out of the room. This fool was smart enough to know that Toya was heading to get her gun. Just as she was reaching to open the drawer, I called her phone. I guess I saved this damn fool's life.

"I'm gon' have to call you back. I'm about to blow Austin's muthafuckin' brains out," Toya said and then hang up the phone. Well, damn! Good thing I am outside her house. Just as I was getting out the car, I see Austin yellow ass running to the car trying to leave. So the first thing I say to myself is, "Aw, this bish was serious!" I got my ass back in the car because bullets ain't got no name on them. Hell, I don't like his ass no way. So I damn sure was not about to get in front of him.

Austin drove away and I saw Toya coming to the door. I rolled my window down and yelled, "Bish, you okay? Can I get out the car?" Instead of her ass giving me an answer, she just looked at me and went back in the house. Mane, I am not about to go in there. So I sent her a text and asked if she was good. As I am waiting on her to respond, I see her come to the door and yell to tell me to bring my ugly ass in the house.

Wayment, Bish! I ain't did nothing to you. But hell, she's got the gun, so I'm just gon' be ugly and whatever else she calls me.

I walked into the house, and this girl is pouring us up a drink. I mean, she has been my best friend for years, and I know how she is when she is this calm. She is mad as hell. It means that she is about to tear some shit up. I really hope Austin don't bring his ass back home no time soon, especially if I am here because my ass does not get involved in domestic disputes.

"This bastard really got me fucked up!" Toya said to me as she sat down with the drinks in front of her.

"So girl, what the hell happened?" I asked but noticing that she got both the cups in front of her. As she is drinking, she's telling me that she was in the shower and Austin came to join her. She expressed how she was kind of happy because they haven't done anything intimate in a while. So for him to join her in the shower, she just knew she was about to get a little DQuel. Now the story gets juicy and my eyebrows started going up when she tells me that when he turned around to start his shower, there was a condom inside his ass cheeks.

Ok, now I see why she got both of them drinks in front of her. Hell, I was thinking she poured both of us a drink, but come to find out, my girl needed them both. I could see the pain and anger in her eyes and the hurt in her voice. However, I think my friend is kind of clueless on what this mean.

"I got to find out what female he is fucking!" Toya says to me as I'm just looking at her. Okay, I just know that my friend is not that naive that she thinks he is fucking with a *woman*. I ain't the smartest person in the world, but I know damn well that no woman can wear a condom, and I'm trying to figure out how it got stuck in his ass if he sleeping with a woman. I just think my friend is so upset that she is not even thinking correctly. I want to say something to her, but I think it is best for me to let her calm down a little first. I just tell her to go ahead and get ready and let's go have brunch and mimosas.

As I am waiting in the car for Toya to get ready, I call my girl British.

"Hello?" British answers and almost tries to tell me that she is going to have to call me back.

"Bish, we got to talk, and I got to tell you something quick.

"Okay, can it wait for about 20 minutes? I need to get ready for a home showing.

"Nope, because Austin is sleeping with a man and in 20 minutes, Toya is going to be with me."

"Wait! Hold the hell up. Let me tell these people I am going to be late."

British gets back on the phone and ask me for details. So I am telling her the tea -- giving her the short, rated R version. I am telling her that Toya and Austin were taking a shower and when he turned around, Toya pulled a condom from his ass. I also tell British that Toya is being so naive that she is still thinking that he is sleeping with a woman and seems to have no clue that only a man will be sticking a condom in ass.

British was speechless and that never happens. I told her that we were going to brunch and that she should meet us there but had to get off the phone because Toya was walking to the car.

As we were riding, Toya was kind of quiet. I noticed that she was on Austin's FaceBook page, and it looked like she was trying to figure out who he was sleeping with. I grabbed her phone and told her that she is just making herself feel worse.

"I just need to know. I just need to know why he is even cheating. We have been together forever, and why is there a need for him to even cheat? If he didn't want to be with me and wanted to be with another woman, he could have just told me." Toya just kept going on and on.

I know she is hurt and she is venting, but it has to stop because she is making herself upset over nothing because Austin is most definitely not sleeping with a woman. I hope that once she calms down, she will come to the realization about it. Well hell, at least I hope so anyway.

We pull up to the restaurant and I tell Toya to just leave her phone in the car so she can focus. We get seated and ordered. Soon after, British walks in and sits down. British is a good actress so I knew she would not spill to Toya that I had already informed her of what was going on.

"I didn't know you guys were coming here. Why y'all heffas didn't call me? British asked as she was looking at the menu.

"Oh girl. It was last minute. I felt Toya needed to get out of the house," I said looking at Toya.

British tries to get Toya to tell her what is going on, but Toya just keeps quiet, so British makes her talk.

"Toya, what the hell is wrong with you. I see it all over your face, and I know Maya is waiting for you to say something." British said to Toya.

"Girl I just found out that Austin is cheating on me."

"What? Are you serious? How do you know? With who?" British kept going before she was interrupted my Toya.

Toya looked at British and told her that she has no clue who the woman is, but she has known for some time now that Austin was cheating on her and that she finally has confirmation.

"What happened, girl?" British asked as she is drinking her mimosa.

Toya goes on with the spill and tries to hold back the tears. To British, it was a replay in her head. She knew that feeling all too well.

It was just a few months ago when she was in Toya's seat, and she was trying to hold back the tears. British takes Toya by the hand and tells her that she knows how she is feeling, and that she is going to make sure that she helps her get over it. I take Toya's other hand to let her know that I am here to beat whomever's ass we need to beat. See, this is the time where we need a good old girl's day. We are getting ready to take over Vegas for Sade's wedding weekend. This will definitely be one to remember, because everyone is coming on this trip, even Ricky. Yes, Ricky! I *had* to invite my ace, because even when I am on vacation, I am working. We just never know when there will be *tea* in the city, so we are always on the READY.

As we are getting ready to leave, Toya spots Austin getting out of his car in valet outside of the restaurant. Her little yellow face instantly turned red. British was always so calm, but of course she does not want to say anything to Toya because she knew how she acted the day she cut the fuck up with Jordan when she found out he had been cheating.

Austin walked in and saw Toya. He walked up to the table, without speaking to British or me. He asked Toya if he could speak with her.

"Well hey, you little cheating fucker," I looked up at him and said.

Austin kind of nodded his head at me and waited for Toya to answer.

"Whatever you need to say, you can say in front of my girls, because you just might need them to save your ass," Toya replied as she sipped her drink.

Austin rolled his eyes and said, "Don't worry about it, I'll just see your little childish ass at home."

Aww I just know this bastard didn't. Before I could call him a bitch, Toya had taken the bottle that was sitting on the table and hit Austin across the head.

"Bish, we just paid $28 for that bottle," I yelled out. Toya just walked over Austin and headed for the door.

British stepped over his bitch ass and went after Toya. I saw a $50 bill sticking out his back pocket. So before stepping over his ass, I snatched it. Hell, he gon' pay for brunch today. Everyone in the restaurant just looking and wondering what the hell was going on. I just keep walking and yelled out, "She caught him cheating. He aight. Y'all can go back to enjoying your day."

On the ride home, Toya was talking as if she didn't just bust Austin's head. This is just too funny to me.

British left her truck at the restaurant and hopped in the car with us. Toya told us that she can't wait to go to Vegas because she is about to be just like British was when we were in Hawaii. Fuck a light skinned dude.

British and I just start to laugh at Toya because she don't even sound right talking about she is about to fuck another man.

When we arrive at Toya's and she gets out of the car, she tells us that she is about to relive a scene from the movie *Waiting to Exhale.* So tell the neighbors not to call the fire department. I don't know if we need to stay and keep this girl calm or just leave and let her destroy all of his shit. Before walking into the house, she told British to go ahead and make an offer on the home they had looked at.

"Naw, Bish! We keeping *this* house. Let that fucker find somewhere else to stay. We taking him for everything he got. Ain't another nobody about to enjoy this house you built," British yelled back to Toya.

The Betrayal

Whewww, Chile!!!! Are y'all ready for this chapter? Take a few moments and get your favorite drink, because you are about to really be at the edge of your seat. Vegas get real turnt up, and shit started to hit the fan. Make sure you have cleared your day, because you are about to get this last little enjoyment. Buckle up and prepare for takeoff.

****

"OMG Baby! The time has finally come. We are about to get married," Sade jumps up and down yelling to Chad. "Baby we are about to spend a wonderful weekend with our close family and friends and then when we return, we will be husband and wife."

Sade and Chad have been engaged for quite some time now. Sade always knew that Chad was the one she wanted to spend the rest of her life with, but because she was watching her friends' marriages fall apart, she was just not in a rush to be married. Chad never pressured her into getting married either, although he used to always tell her that they shouldn't compare their relationship to anyone's else.

Sade and Chad got up to finish their last little packing before heading to the airport. They are actually going to Vegas a day before everyone else. While Sade is getting ready, she calls me. I love my little baby, but she knows damn well that 10 a.m. is too early to be calling.

"Wake up Bish!" Sade says when I answered.

"Girl what do you want? Shouldn't you be focusing on getting to that airport on time rather than all on my phone waking me up this early," I reply to her getting up checking my notifications on my phone trying to see if I missed something.

Sade is just a yapping away, and all while she is talking, I am reading a text message from Ricky saying that he don't think he is going to Vegas. I interrupt Sade's speech and tell her that I am going to call her back because I needed to call and see what is going on with Ricky. Sade is just so damn spoiled she wants all the talk time. I just rolled my eyes and told the little heffa to hold on so I can call Ricky's ugly ass on a 3-way call.

"See Bish, I knew you was gon' call me and try to talk me into going," Ricky answers the phone and says to me.

"Okay, so what is going on that you don't want to go to Vegas? Mane, don't forget that I bought your ticket, and I don't waste money. And you are damn sure not going to save that ticket for another time and go to Vegas without me," I replied. Hell, I don't know what is going on with Ricky. For the past few weeks, he has just been acting so weird. There has never been a time when he does not want to go on a free trip, and there is never a time when he does not want to be up under *my* ass. I know this fool like a book, and I know there is something that he is just not telling me.

"Hey Ricky. So tell me why you don't want to come spend my wedding weekend with me," Sade asked.

"So you brought Sade into this conversation?" Ricky laughingly says. "Fuck it! I'm going. I ain't even about to argue with Sade's spoiled ass."

I tell Sade to have a safe flight and I will see her tomorrow in Vegas. We all get off the phone and I take my ass back to sleep.

On the other side of town, lies British ole 'in-love' ass. British and Jordan have been separated for months now, but he still will *not* sign the papers to give her a divorce -- although, he got 2 babies on the way and still out here running the streets like the old broke hoe that he is.

British has been with Jayden since leaving Jordan, and everything seems to be going good for them. But of course, he is married as well, and the word is his wife won't give him a divorce either. I just don't see why these people will not sign divorce papers if they are not wanted. Ain't no damn way I am going to force someone to be with me, let alone stay married to me and they don't want my ass. Jayden seems to be cool and British seem to be really happy with his little sexy bald-headed ass. He's a police officer, and he done came into British's life and immediately arrested her heart.

As the sun starts to shine in the wide-open windows in British's bedroom, Jayden rolls over and starts kissing British as she sleeps. The love he has shown her since day one is just so wonderful. It's something that she needed in her life. Jayden would always go to sleep with his music playing from his phone. So he woke up to a song on his playlist that reminded him of the love he and British have. As the song starts to play, he began singing it in British's ear. Of course, British has always been a hard sleeper so she ain't heard nothing. But Jayden didn't care that she really didn't know what was going on. He loved British enough to still show his love for her even when she does not see it.

She finally wakes up, and she rolls over to see that Jayden is just looking at her.

"Good Morning babe. Why are you just staring? Is something wrong?" British asks Jayden.

"No, you were sleeping so good that you didn't even realize that I had been singing to you in your ear," Jayden replies.

British just looks at Jayden and smiles. She always say to herself that she is glad she chose to hang around that night with Nikki, because she has finally met the one true love who she feels will not do the things she experienced in her marriage. It is like he was created just for her. They have fun, they travel, they stay up all night talking on the phone when they are not together. They make sure they have lunch time together during the week and so much more. I am just glad that my friend is finally happy. I mean if she can ever get this divorce over with, I wouldn't be surprised if she is married again soon after--although she always says that she is not getting married anymore.

British is the one person that when she loves, she loves hard. Her tolerance is very low, but she is very loyal in her relationship when she knows that she has loyalty in return. From the little time that we have been around Jayden, we all love him for British. It seems as if he completes her, gives her hope that all men are not the same, gives her the time she needs to heal and find herself. But he also shows her the love she needs to feel and fills that void she had in her heart.

"Baby, I am so ready for this vacation with you," British says to Jayden as she gets up and heads to take a shower.

"Yea, I know. We both need this vacation baby," Jayden replies as he follows British into the bathroom.

They take their shower together. The shower always begins with kissing, fucking, and then cleaning their bodies. They finish and start to get ready for their day. British has two clients to meet to show homes, and Jayden is working a double shift since he is going on vacation.

Both British and Jayden are successful in their careers. British is the top real estate agent in the city and Jayden is a detective with the police force. They say their goodbyes and head out the door.

Two blocks down the street is Nikki's uncommitted ass. She has been having a lot of fun lately with someone she has been secretly dating. You never know what Nikki is doing because one thing about her, she is not going to reveal who she is talking to or who she is fucking. Nikki is already awake, because unlike the rest of us, she decided to leave for Vegas a day early as well-- not to be with Sade, but to spend some time with Phil before the rest of us arrive. No one still knows that Nikki and Phil have been seeing each other since our trip to Hawaii. Phil is in Vegas for a Conference with his job. It was perfect for Nikki because she can have some sex time even while she is in Vegas. Phil left a few days ago, and Nikki was getting ready to head to the airport. While getting her bags trying to hurry and leave to make it to the airport, she gets a call from British.

"Hello?" Nikki answers

"Good Morning, Bish! What you up to?" British asks.

"Oh! Nothing girl. Just finished packing and probably just lay around the house and relax today.

"Girl please! I am about to pull up over there because I need to talk to you about something."

"Can it wait? Girl I really need to get some things done around this house before Vegas."

Nikki tries to do everything possible to keep British from popping up at her house, simply because she only had 2 hours to get to the airport and she knew that eventually she would be getting a call from Phil, and the last thing she wants to happen is to get a phone call from Phil while she is around British. So she quickly thinks to herself that she will just have to let British come and get whatever she needs to say out. Then she will rush her ass out so she can secretly head to the airport without anyone knowing.

British finally arrives at Nikki and before she could knock on the door, Nikki was opening the door.

"Come on in Bish so we can get this over with!" Nikki said pulling British inside the door. "What did Jordan do now? Or did you find something out about Jayden? Or hell, did Jordan and Jayden meet? Like hurry the hell up because I got ish to do!"

"Girl shut the hell up. You ain't got no more to do than the rest of us before leaving for Vegas," British says to Nikki as she goes to Nikki's bar and pours herself a drink.

British sits down on the couch and tells Nikki that she is really bugging about Phil. She advises Nikki that Phil had sent her a text message and that she hasn't been able to stop thinking about him since. Of course Nikki is really puzzled because she is trying to figure out why the fuck would Phil be sending British a message if she is the one who has been fucking him.

British goes on to say that she sent Phil a friend request on Facebook the night she found his profile and that they had been exchanging messages since a few days after. Damn Nikki. I guess you ain't the only one who is getting played...kind of fucked up that Nikki has been thinking she is playing her *own* best friend for a man, and come to find out, she is the one who is getting played. Okay, so let me finish with the story...

"You didn't tell me that you and Phil were talking," Nikki says to Brit.

"Well hell, I've been trying to tell you since that day, but you been so busy with this new secret man that you been seeing that you ain't had time for my tea," British responds.

Nikki is just boiling on the inside and although she wants to go the fuck off, she knows that it is not British's fault because she has no idea that she and Phil have been seeing each other.

British starts to show Nikki texts and pictures messages from Phil. Turns out, Phil has been sending British dick pictures and has also been trying to get her to meet him for sex. At this point, Nikki cannot *wait* to get to Vegas to call Phil out on his shit.

"Girl, he is just so damn fine, and it has been so tempting not to go fuck him," British says.

"But girl, I did meet him for drinks the other night just to see what he was talking about, and we almost fucked at the damn bar."

"Oh! Details Bish. I want all the details," Nikki says while taking shot after shot of liquor and watching the clock to make sure she doesn't miss getting to the airport.

Eventually, British gets a call from Jayden and leaves. Nikki couldn't get her stuff and get to the airport fast enough. As she is heading to the airport, she gets a call from Phil. She tries her best to hold herself together because she does not want Phil to know that British has spilled the tea on his lying ass. She tells him that she is kind of running late and that she will see him when she gets to Vegas.

Right down the street is Toya and Austin's dysfunctional asses. Toya and Austin have not said two words to each other since finding out he's been cheating. Toya has filed for a divorce and is just waiting on a court date since they can't agree on anything. Austin wants the house, but Toya ain't going. She refuses to allow another bitch to live in the house that she built. I mean, I can't argue with that. What she don't know, is she really don't have to worry about a *bitch* moving in. She got to worry about what *man* is moving in. Oh well, she still hasn't figured out that her husband is actually gay. So let's just move on...

Toya hates the fact that she has to go on this trip with Austin, but he is actually singing at the wedding. He has to be there. Toya has in her mind that she is going to be on some bald head hoe ish. This crazy ass lady done went and cut her hair and everything. See, that's why I am so glad that I am single. These men be having these women cutting their hair and just doing all kinds of crazy stuff.

"Toya, I really think it is a good idea for us to get along on this trip and continue to wear our rings for Sade and Chad's sake. We don't want them to know that we are divorcing," Austin says to Toya.

"Boy, Fuck you! I ain't gon' be caught near your trifling ass," Toya responds and walks downstairs leaving him standing in their bedroom looking stupid.

A car pulls up outside and Toya kisses and tells the boys good-bye. Austin didn't know that Toya changed her flight and booked another hotel so she would not have to be with him. The only other flight she could get was one that was leaving a day before. Apparently, Austin has been too tied up hoeing around. He hasn't even noticed that Toya has completely charged that American Express Black card up. My girl ain't playing with that ass.

Lastly, we have my stupid ass sister, Dani. She kind of been MIA simply because she is five months pregnant, and Sade knows about her and Jordan and her pregnancy. Sade made it perfectly clear that she did not want Dani in her wedding anymore, but she didn't say that she could not come to the wedding. Dani actually hasn't spoken to Sade since they met at the restaurant, and Dani kind of feels some type of way about still going to Vegas. Like everyone else, the trip was planned months ago, and tickets were already purchased so even if she doesn't go to the wedding, at least she will have a good trip.

Dani and Kendall have still been seeing each other. He knows about her pregnancy and has chosen to still be with her. She was pregnant before he was in the picture. Although he knows about the pregnancy, he has no idea that she is pregnant by her best friend's husband. All he knows is that the father bounced and has not been in the picture. So he was not about to let Dani go through this alone. What a good man he is. If only Dani could've found him before she got wrapped up into Jordan's manipulating ass. Dani is actually scared to say anything to Kendall because she feels that he will judge her and leave her.

I do check on my sister quite often because I know it is tough going through what she is going through. I wish she would just come clean about everything so she can have a stress-free pregnancy. At least when she comes clean, she will only have to worry about losing British as a friend and not British whooping her ass. British has a temper out this world, and although it takes a lot to get her to that level, she is a beast when she does. Vegas is about to be really interesting.

Kendall comes into Dani's bedroom with breakfast. He opens the curtains and gives her the forehead kiss. Dani knows she has a good man and that is why she is just so afraid of losing him. She hopes that she has placed a mark on him so that when he does find out the truth, he will love her enough to stay.

"Baby, you are absolutely the best. I don't know what I did to deserve you, but I am not questioning it," Dani says to him.

"I know it has only been a short time, but I love you Dani, and I know it was fate that brought us together," Kendall responds.

"I am so looking forward to this wonderful weekend with you baby!" Dani says with excitement.

As Kendall gets up, he informs Dani that he has planned some time with his family, and he wants her to meet them. His family lives in California, which is only a few hours from Vegas, so he has arranged for a rental car to drive to California after their time in Vegas. Kendall booked their plane tickets, so Dani had no idea that they were flying into Vegas but flying out of California.

"You think they will like me?" Dani asks Kendall as she was looking in the mirror at herself. He comes up behind her and responds, "Of course baby." He kisses her on her neck and just as he was getting ready to walk off Dani ask, "What will they say about me being pregnant and you being with someone who's pregnant with another man's child?"

Before Kendall can respond, he gets a phone call. He picks up his phone and tells Dani that he will be right back. Dani was a bit suspicious, because Kendall never takes calls out of her presence. She instantly starts to think about when Jordan would do the same thing, but she had to quickly remind herself that Kendall is *nothing* like Jordan.

****

Vegas we are here, Baby, and it is about to go down! Everyone has made their arrival and I am just waiting on shit to hit the fan. I mean, even though I am on vacation, I am still working and looking for the next big story to air. Shit, my boss done told me I may be out of a job if I don't start publishing hot topics. So what better city to be in than Vegas. I know y'all waiting on the juicy tales of this trip. Hell, me too. I hope those seatbelts are still tightened because we about to take off. This is your captain speaking. We have reached the drama destination, where you have first class seats to what is about to happen -- the jaw dropping details of secret relationships, hidden secrets, and why the fuck I am still single. I know y'all are probably thinking just don't nobody want my ass, which could be true. But after this tea, I don't even give a damn.

Nikki arrived in Vegas yesterday but ended up having to get a hotel room because she has not heard from Phil since she touched down. She knows his ass is okay, because he has been all over social media. When she landed, she texted him and asked for the hotel details and the driver information. Phil had told Nikki that he had arranged for a car service to pick her up from the airport and then bring her to the hotel. Well, she waited at the airport for hours and no sign of a driver and no response from Phil. So, she went ahead and got an Uber. Stupid of Nikki to not even know the hotel he was staying in, so she didn't even know where the hell to the tell driver to take her. None of the other girls were there but Sade, so she didn't have anyone to call. She called and texted Phil about ten times. He did finally text back, but he replied, "Give me a minute, tied up with something."

"Give you a minute? Mutha Fucker, I done gave you 2 hours," Nikki said out loud after reading his reply. Rather than just waiting around on Phil and getting even more frustrated, she decided to just go to the hotel everyone else was staying at and get a room for the night hoping that she would just talk to Phil and head to the hotel he was staying at.

After checking into the room, she bumps into Sade and Chad. She didn't tell Sade she was coming in early, so it was a surprise to see her.

"Nikki?" Sade says. "What are you doing here so early?"

"Oh, I decided to fly in a day early and do some *me* time at the spa," Nikki replies. She knew she could not tell Sade that she was seeing Phil and that she only came a day early so she could spend some alone time with him.

"So why you didn't tell me? I could've used your hand early today," Sade laughs and say as she gives Nikki a hug.

Nikki steps back and replies, "Yea, Bish, that's why I didn't tell you I was coming early. I just said I came to have some *me* time. Y'all bishes won't let me enjoy myself back at home."

They laughed and parted ways. Nikki went to her room, and Sade and Chad left to handle some last-minute wedding duties.

Nikki got in the room, put her bags down and tried to call Phil one more time. Still no answer. So she sent him a text message.

"So you just gon' have me at the airport waiting for details. I landed hours ago. I didn't know what car service

to look for nor hotel to come to. You were supposed to text me the details. I have called your phone numerous times. You are not that damn busy where you can't at least reply back to me with the details. I guess you don't care about me being out here with nowhere to go."

Just when she was getting ready to get in the shower, she gets a message back from Phil.

"I told you I was busy. Stop fucking calling my phone like you don't know I am here for work. Your friends are here, so go be with them until I call you back."
Nikki looked at her phone in disbelief because she cannot understand why Phil is talking to her the way he is. She thinks to herself that clearly Phil don't know who the fuck she is. He hasn't met the ghetto and hood Nikki. She takes a deep breath and then sends Phil a very nice and nasty response back.

"Clearly you got to be texting the wrong mutha fucker. First off, my friends do not come until tomorrow. Second, it was your idea for me to fly here a day before everyone so we would have some alone time without any interruptions from them. Third, you were the one who said you were setting up a car service to bring me to the *hotel. Fourth, who the fuck you think you talking to. Don't think I can't handle my own shit, but this was all your idea. If you wanted to do something different, you could have very well communicated that to me, and I wouldn't have been sitting at the airport for hour waiting. Fifth, did I ask you already who the hell you think you talking to?"*

By this time Nikki is livid and really wants to know if Phil is on some bullshit. The fact that she does not know what hotel he is staying in is kind of bothering her because she can't find out. So rather than dwelling on his ass, she decided to go ahead and get dressed up and start exploring what the city is offering. "Fuck Phil," Nikki said to herself. "Well I literally do want to fuck him because I am horny as hell…"

Nikki goes out, gets something to eat and finally arrived back at the hotel. Still no call or text from Phil. At this point, she is just calling the night a loss and goes to bed. Good thing she brought her credit card because she was able to book her own room. Thing is, she only booked it for one night, so she's hoping to hear from Phil before check out time.

All throughout the night, she checks her phone to see if Phil had called or texted her. At this point, she is beyond confused as to why the sudden change in Phil from just a few days ago. So she decided that once she checks out in the morning, she is going to call every last hotel until she finds the one he is in.

It is 11:20 a.m., and everyone is beginning to roll on into Vegas and check into the hotel. Sade and Chad have spent that last few days making sure everything is in order for their friends who are coming in for their wedding. Everyone is staying at the same hotel so we can all be together. That was one thing Sade requested when she sent out the invites.

Sade and Chad have set up the first night to be a Meet and Greet so both sides can meet each other. They have asked all their guests to wear luau attire for the first night and all black for their wedding. The luau theme idea comes from Hawaii since Chad actually proposed to Sade the year they went to Hawaii for her birthday.

Not sure why they asked for all black for the wedding though... It's probably a good thing because there just may be a funeral with all the ish that is about to hit the fan while we are here in Vegas.

British and Jayden are the first couple to arrive. As soon as they walk into the hotel, they run into Jordan and Chad as they are walking out. British knew that it would be no way to avoid Jordan this weekend since he is Chad's best man, but the thought of seeing him every time she turns around is something she does not plan on doing. British tries her best to walk another way to keep Jordan from approaching her, but he always like to do shit for attention.

"Hey Brit!" Chad says to British as he gives her a hug

"Hey bro! Are you ready?" British responds to Chad

"Ready as I'm gon' get," Chad then says as he heads over to speak to Jayden.

"What's up man? I'm glad you came." Chad shakes Jayden's hand.

"Congrats man!" Jayden says as he heads over to the front desk to check him and British in.

As British stands to the side and waits on Jayden, Jordan did not waste any time to get in her space.

"What the fuck do you want?" British says to Jordan as she rolls her eyes.

Jordan really does miss British, but he knows that he has done so much fucked up shit to her in the past, along with the fact that she is entertaining someone else, he really thinks it is over for him this time.

"I just want to tell you that you look beautiful in that dress," Jordan says to British as he tries to grab her by her arm.

"If you don't get your ass back before I slap the hell out of you." British grabs her things and heads in Jayden's direction.

Chad laughs at Jordan and tells him to come on and leave British alone. Jordan has done so much in the past and has always been able to just start being sweet and say he's sorry and British would give in and forgive him. Does he really think that he has another shot at making it right with British? Dumb ass don't see that she is actually *happy* with Jayden and is not thinking about his ass.

As Chad and Jordan head to the hotel bar, Jordan spots Dani walking up the steps.

"Daaaaammmn!!!! Jordan says as he looks at Dani.

"What mane?" Chad turns around and ask Jordan.

"Look at my other fine piece of ass coming in now," Jordan responds as he tries to head Dani's way. What Jordan doesn't realize is that Dani is actually not alone. She brought Kendall with her.

Jordan has not seen or spoken with Dani since she told him that she was pregnant. Of course, he wanted Dani to have an abortion. And although Dani knows that the situation is fucked up -- having an affair with her best friend's husband and getting pregnant -- she does not believe in killing. So, when Dani told Jordan that she was keeping the baby, he got ghost. Jordan has no idea that Dani has been seeing Kendall since then and that he has stepped up to help Dani take care of the baby.

"Hey beautiful. I miss you," Jordan says as he stands behind Dani and kisses her on her neck.

"Bye Jordan," Dani says as she moves away from him because she knows Kendall is not far behind her.

"Don't act like you ain't happy to see me. I'm in room 3468. Bring me some of that pregnant pussy tonight." He licks his lips expecting Dani to say okay.

Dani looks at Jordan and laughs. "Sorry, the only person getting some of this pregnant pussy is my man. Now bye Jordan." Dani walks away.

"Mane damn! Looks like your women ain't fucking with you," Chad laughs as he hits Jordan on the back.

"Mane please. British is my wife, and as long as I'm her husband, she ain't going nowhere because I ain't signing no papers. And Dani is pregnant with my baby, so I am entitled to that ass," Jordan responds as he puts on his shades and walks back towards the bar.

Then my sexy ass and Ricky walk in. I ain't got no hoes, so wasn't nobody waiting on me to walk through the door. I just got Ricky's single ass, and he don't even like coochie. We check in and get ready to scope out the hotel and then the city for some juicy tea.

As I am talking to Ricky, I notice that his attention is somewhere else.

"Uh Rick. You don't hear me talking to you?" I ask Ricky as he is looking in the direction of the hotel lobby.

"Yea, I see him over there," Ricky responds to me, but of course he has no idea what I just said to him.

"You see who over there?" I asked.

"Austin."

"Who in the hell looking for Austin?"

"Huh? No, I thought you asked was that Austin over there."

Now why in the hell would I be asking about Austin? I don't even like that fool.

Okay, so Ricky is acting real suspicious. Aw hell naw! Don't tell me!!! Wait a whole damn minute. Please don't tell me that Ricky and Austin are fucking. Ain't no way! Now I know I am not the smartest person in the world, but I think I just found out who Austin is fucking.

"So Rick! Why are you staring at Austin like that?" I ask as we are getting on the elevator.

"Girl what? Why would I be staring at that married man like that?" Rick responds to me trying his best not to look at me in my eyes.

"Bish! How long y'all been fucking?" I just came out and say.

"Maya really?" Ricky can barely even say with a straight face.

"Don't lie to me. You gon' tell me all these details when we get in this room." I push the number of the floor we are on and couldn't wait to get to our room to get this tea.

When we finally get in the room and I throw them bags to the side, I tell Ricky to spill it. He couldn't help but come clean with me. He tells me that he and Austin ran into each other at Target and it was a day that he had just left the gym, so he had his work out shorts on. He says that Austin started making flirty comments about his shorts and told him that he needed to start working out because he had started to gain weight. Ricky told him where he worked out at and advised him that he goes running every morning at the park. Austin told Ricky that he would meet him the next morning to go running. Ricky tells me that he didn't think nothing of it, but it all changed during their run. As they were running, they ran through a hidden trail that no one could see. Ricky tells me that Austin stops and say that he needed a break to catch his breath. So they both stopped. While Ricky was leaning over, Austin comes up behind him and put his cucumber on it. As I am listening to this story, all I can think about is Toya telling me that Austin had started going running in the mornings and all of a sudden got the interest into working out.

Ricky continues on to tell me that he turned around and they started kissing and fucked on the leaning tree. From what Ricky tells me, they have been intimate for 6 months.

I just could not believe what I was hearing. Now I see why Ricky did not want to come around when Toya was present. He was sleeping with her husband. Of course, he tells me to promise that I won't tell Toya. I tell him that they gon' stop putting me in these situations where I got to choose between not telling my best friends about their men and my job. See this is why I don't care to be in a relationship. Hell, now-a-days you don't know if you in a relationship with a man or a bitch...

Toya walks in and the first person she sees is Austin. She looks at him in pure disgust. Since he is standing with the fellas, he tries to play it off and goes over to help Toya with her bags.

"Get your hoe ass back," Toya yells out loud where everyone pretty much heard her.

"Baby, don't do this on Sade and Chad's weekend." Austin tries to whisper to Toya.

"Hey y'all! Will y'all please come and get y'all's cheating ass friend?" She says to the guys as she walks away and checks in at the hotel desk.

As Austin is walking back towards the guys, Jordan holler out and say, "Mane, what you get caught doing?" Austin just shakes his head and orders him a drink and tell the guys that this is going to be a very long weekend.

Well it's almost time for Sade and Chad's pre-wedding Luau event. Everyone arrives and looks so colorful. The event is taking place at the hotel where we are staying along with other corporate events in other ballrooms, so the hotel is full of folks tonight. As always, I am the first to arrive because I am trying to see if I can catch a story.

British and Jayden walk in first. British has on this pretty, colorful high low dress that is fitting all of her curves. Jayden has on this nice linen outfit with the pocket scarf to match British's dress. OMG, they look so cute together.

Next walks in Nikki looking colorful and lonely. She has on a fuchsia body con dress. We all know she wears this type of attire to as bait to prey on her next victim.

Toya comes in right after Nikki. She really looks like she doesn't even care how she came -- no thought into her attire at all. Her country ass got on a dress that looks like she pulled it out of the Goodwill.

Lastly, Dani and Kendall come in. Dani looks so pretty in her luau maternity sundress. I guess Jordan is following her because he nearly walks in with them with his shirt all open looking like a damn fool. I really can't believe that Dani came to the event, but I guess she feels like Sade won't say anything and ruin her event. All the guys come in together and finally Sade and Chad arrive.

As everyone is sitting at the table, Sade and Chad is going around hugging and thanking the guests for coming. Thank God our table is last because I just cannot wait to see what her reaction is going to be when she gets to our table and sees that Dani is here.

I love when we are all together just talking and having a good time. It's never a dull moment when Jordan is somewhere near. Nobody in the circle really cares for him but the guys. He is just not a likable person. If ain't nobody else glad British left him, I sure am.

As we are talking, all of a sudden everyone's phones start blowing up with tags and comments from social media. I look at my phone, and I just could not believe my eyes. "What the fuck?" I say out loud. Everyone is looking at me, and I am trying to figure out how this story got out. I look at British and I can just see the embarrassment in her eyes and all I want her to know is that I had nothing to do with it.

"You bitch!" British says as she looks at me with pure disappointment.

"British I did not have anything to do with this," I say as I am just trying to see how anyone could get a hold to the story about Jordan and the stripper.

"Bitch, it has your name under the article. How the fuck you didn't do it?" British replies.

Right there, the complete story of Jordan and Monese has surfaced, and it is all over the internet. As I look around the table, all I can see is everyone looking at me shaking their head. I try my best to explain that I had nothing to do with it. Nikki looks at me and asks why would anyone post a story and put my name on it, and she asks if the story was true. All I could do was answer yes.

"The story was on my computer, but I did not release it. I promise. Brit, I would not do you like that," I said.

"Yes you did, trick. You have always been jealous of British *and* our marriage. So you couldn't wait to destroy it," Jordan says to me leaning back drinking his drink.

"Jealous of y'all's marriage? Negro, please. Y'all marriage ain't never been nothing but pure bullshit," I reply to Jordan.

British sits her drink down and had the audacity to ask me, "I mean were you? I know your broke ass was looking for a story because your boss was threatening to fire you because you have been off your game."

"Look, I didn't have anything to do with this. Nobody has access to my laptop but..." I stop and look at Ricky. Ricky is drinking on his drink looking all stupid.

"Bitch! It was you. You did this. You asked to use my laptop because you left yours at home. You stole this information off my laptop," I angrily say to Ricky as I got up to slap the fuck out of him. I just cannot believe my very own friend and assistant would do that.

Ricky got up and said, "Mane, whatever. British is your friend, not mines. I wasn't about to be on the street because you are saving someone who knew she was married to a hoe anyway."

"You fagget mutha fucker," Jordan says as he gets up and walks toward Ricky but was instantly stopped by Austin.

"So you got a stripper pregnant Jordan?" Dani asks Jordan. Everyone is going back and forth which is when Sade and Chad notice that something is going wrong. As they walk over to our table, Dani is the first person Sade sees.

"Why the fuck are you here?" Sade asks. Dani just wants to get up and leave at that point. She looks up at

Sade and tells her that she is sorry and that she will just leave. As she is getting her purse, Kendall takes her hand and ask why would her best friend not want her to be in attendance at her wedding event. Dani replies to Kendall and says that it is a long story, and she would tell him later and it was time to leave.

I am just so over all these secrets, so it is time for us to bury them and move on. I tell Dani to sit down and face whatever she is about to face. While Dani sits back down, Sade yells out, "Naw, Bitch. Get up, get your shit and whoever husband this is and get your ass up out of here. Everyone is looking at the both of them and just cannot understand why Sade is talking to Dani like she is. Chad takes Sade by her hand and tries to remove her from the table so they can enjoy the rest of their party. Sade is over it.

"Okay, so you want to stay? Fine. You can stay but you got to tell your supposed *best friend* who you are pregnant by," Sade says to Dani.

Dani's mouth just drops, and she feels as if her heart is being yanked from her chest. All you can see are tears coming from her eyes as she looks at Kendall hoping that he will understand that all of this was a mistake and not who she really is. Kendall has this confused look on his face and seem as he needs to stick around for the answer.

"So it's you who my husband cheating with? You bitch," Toya yells out as she throws her drink at Dani.

"Girl, what? Ain't nobody sleeping with your gay ass husband but Ricky's sissy ass," Dani blurts out. Okay, yes. I kind of mentioned to my sister what I had found out, but I didn't think it was gon' come out so soon. I had gone to go visit my sister in her room, and we just got to talking. Aw damn! I told y'all Vegas was about to reveal some shit.

"Wait what?" Toya looks at Austin and then Ricky and damn near throws up.

"So, if Toya's husband is fucking a man then the only husband left is Jordan," Nikki says as she looks over at British.

"Which means you are pregnant by my husband," British says as the tears start flowing down her face. This shit just can't get any worse.

"British, I am so sorry. I didn't mean for this to happen. It just happened," Dani tries to explain.

Jordan laughs and responds, "Just happened? You told me I was married to the wrong woman and you were supposed to be the wife. You came onto me for years before I fucked you. It didn't just happen. You wanted it to happen."

"So you got pregnant by my husband then turned around and asked me if I would be your child's godmother? Bitch you really need help." British gets up and tell Jayden that she was ready to go.

Jordan tried to go after British to try and explain, but he was immediately stopped in his tracks by Jayden.

"I mean chill, dude. This here is my problem now. You've done enough," Jayden says as he takes British's hand and walk towards the door.

Still sitting at the table, Toya looks at Austin and say, "So the reason why a condom was stuck in your ass is because you had a dick going in it?"

Austin was kind of fucked up because Toya was loud as hell and all the attention was on him. The guys just got up and moved away from him. Austin tries to tell

Toya that it is not what she thinks, but she wasn't trying to hear what Austin was saying, so she leaves.

What a night! Kendall is over all the drama and leaves Dani at the table. Dani just sits at the table crying her eyes out and can't believe what just happened. She knows that Kendall is going to leave her now. She was planning on telling Kendall about the entire situation. She was just waiting until the time was right. I always told my sister that no time was right and that she should have told Kendall the truth in the beginning.

It looks like Sade and Chad's luau party has officially been ruined. Sade just stands in the middle of the floor and looks at Chad and say, "You see why I was so scared to get married? Let me find out you fucked one of them and see don't I kill you." She walks away and leaves Chad just standing by himself. Chad goes after Sade and stops her, "Baby, you ain't got to worry about me sleeping with none of them because they ghetto as fuck." They both laughed. "But for real, Boo, I love you.

Fuck a wedding. Let's just go get married with just our parents." Sade could not agree with him more.

As we all were walking out and headed back to our rooms, we see Nikki in the lobby going the fuck off. Couldn't really see who she was going off on because whoever the dude was, he was walking away from Nikki on the arm of another woman.

"Phil, you act like you don't see me standing here calling your fucking name?" Nikki says as she takes her shoes off and runs after him.

Phil? I think to myself. I look over at British and see her in disbelief. Poor British. She has just gotten hit with all type of news this weekend. She turns and look at Jayden and tells him that the best part of this weekend is that she is glad that she is spending with the one person that erases all the negative shit from her mind. He replies and tells her that she should choose her besties more wisely. They laugh and head to their room. Meanwhile, I stand in the lobby and just can't believe this happened. I don't think Vegas was ready for this type of action.

Sade and Chad go ahead and get married at a chapel in a private ceremony with just their parents; we find out that Toya is married to an undercover gay man; Dani still ends up having to deal with her pregnancy alone. What's so messed up is that Kendall was planning on proposing to Dani at his parent's house; Nikki is just as fucked up and trifling as Dani and was sleeping with guys that British has been with; and British seem to be the true friend that just may be the one who ends up happy. Well at least we hope she does anyway. The way her night has been going, she just may not be done with surprises.

****

I think it is safe to say that this college friendship could very well be over. I mean how could it not? Who can recover from something like this? You got one girl pregnant by her best friend's husband, another girl who was sleeping behind that same best friend's back with her island sex buddy, one girl who finds out that her husband is gay, and another girl who wants to whoop all of their asses. Yep, this friendship is over.

This night has been so draining. I am just ready to go to bed. Walking to the elevator, I see Nikki coming down the hallway with all her luggage. She explains to me that she was supposed to be staying in the room with Phil but turns out he came to Vegas to be with someone else. So basically, her ass ain't got nowhere to go because the hotel is absolutely booked the rest of the weekend.

"Come on bish! But you giving me half on this high ass room. Ricky's ass can stay in the room with his boo," I say to Nikki trying to help her get all her damn bags.

As British and Jayden are walking and holding hands, British can't help but feel like she is safe in Jayden's arms. Just in a matter of minutes, she was hit with so much from the people who she thought loved her. Being married to a cheater was hard enough, but to find out that he got two women pregnant and one being her best friend was horrific. She just wanted to get to the room and make love to Jayden and forget that this night ever happened. British lays her head on Jayden and he whispers to her, "I'm about to tear that ass up tonight." He takes out the room key and opens the door. British walks in to see a woman sitting on the bed.

"Who the hell is this?" She says as she looks at the woman.

"Fuck!" Jayden says as he put his hand over his face. "This is my wife, Amber"

"Okay God, if it ain't nobody out there for me just tell me," British says as she throws her hand up in the air and walks out of the room.

Just when she thought that Jayden could make her forget about what her friends had just put her through, she is instantly hit with the reality that he is married!

Poor British. She is *Married to a Cheater and in love with a Husband!*